ZOCOCA
THE MEXICAN BANDIT

ZOCOCA
THE MEXICAN BANDIT

The infamous Mexican bandit Zococa and his mute Apache sidekick Tahoka were broke but who would hire them? The answer lay in the border town of Rio Concho, where the pair were offered $1,000 to kill a young rancher, although Zococa certainly had no intention of killing anyone in cold blood. Intrigued by the assignment, Zococa and Tahoka headed off to the intended victim's smallholding, only to hear a beautiful woman in distress. Zococa investigated and that was when the trouble really started. Soon the bandits were enticed into a tangled web of intrigue, with death stalking them at every step.

Zococa The Mexican Bandit

by

Michael D. George

Dales Large Print Books
Long Preston, North Yorkshire,
BD23 4ND, England.

British Library Cataloguing in Publication Data.

George, Michael D.
  Zococa the Mexican bandit.

  A catalogue record of this book is
  available from the British Library

  ISBN   1-84262-147-5 pbk

First published in Great Britain in 2001 by Robert Hale Limited

Copyright © Michael D. George 2001

Cover illustration © Ballestar by arrangement with
Norma Editorial

The right of Michael D. George to be identified as the author of
this work has been asserted by him in accordance with the
Copyright, Designs and Patents Act, 1988

Published in Large Print 2002 by arrangement with
Robert Hale Limited

Published in Large Print ... Library Magna Bo...)ks Ltd.

Printed and bound ...
T.J. (International) Ltd., Cornwall, PL28 8RW

Dedicated to
Tim, Roy, Susan and Abby

PROLOGUE

Luis Santiago Rodrigo Vallencio was no name for a notorious bandit, but being the greatest left-handed shot either side of the long Texas/Mexico border, he had earned himself the more memorable and apt nickname of Zococa. For most of his adult life he had skimmed the law by doing what he did best, being a highly paid gunfighter. At some point during his many excursions back and forth over the border he had become an outlaw with a price upon his head. Exactly how or why seemed to matter little to the man who quite enjoyed being known as a bandit. His incessant bragging did little to clear his name of false charges but added an element of excitement to his life. Zococa also found it gave him a glamorous image which went down well with the fairer sex.

Besides his extraordinary genius with his pistol, Zococa had one other thing he did extremely well, he talked. Not the way most men talk, but continuously and with a flair only found in those of a proud Latin disposition. Zococa had the ability to turn half a dozen pursuers into an even score once he had found a willing audience.

Yet for all his exaggerations, he had never knowingly harmed anyone who did not deserve his fate. He had never cheated an honest man and only took advantage of those who would willingly cheat him given half a chance. If Zococa had two flaws in his nature, one was his total inability to take anything, including himself, seriously. His smile was famed as much as his ability with his prized silver-plated gun. Both dazzled all who came close enough to take note.

Zococa's other weakness was his enjoyment in being the eternal romantic who prided himself on always showering a beautiful face with as many flowers and compliments as were necessary to capture even the most fleeting of kisses. This had cost him dearly on more than one occasion, yet he had always survived with his smile intact.

There were some who said the flamboyant bandit even smiled whilst he was asleep. Only one person could testify to whether this claim was correct, and he would never tell. His name was Tahoka.

Tahoka was an unusually tall, well-built Apache brave who had been saved from the clutches of certain death twelve years earlier by Zococa. The bandit had found the massive man staked out across an ant hill with his tongue ripped from his mouth. Who had done this, or why, to the quiet-natured Indian had never been fully established.

All that was certain was that Tahoka had remained close to the colourful bandit ever since. They had become like brothers as they outwitted and evaded the law almost daily. How the Indian had managed to retain his sanity as he listened to the endless boasting of his friend, was also legendary. Some said the Indian had gone deaf under the incessant verbal assault. Whatever the truth was, there was no more loyal friend than Tahoka.

Whenever Tahoka wished to say anything he would have to interrupt and use hand signals to inform the bandit of what he was thinking. Zococa had a way of making even these rare hand gestures appear unimportant.

Life was for living. Mere existence, to Zococa, was worse than death itself.

Outwitting yet another posse, the two

riders found themselves one day outside a small town called Rio Concho, set just inside Texas on the border with Mexico. A town they knew well.

Zococa decided to see if his unique talents and reputation might prove tempting to anyone willing to hire him. The smiling bandit knew there was always someone eager to hire the notorious Zococa.

What Zococa did not know was how dangerous a web he was riding into.

ONE

There was a look on the face of the bounty hunter which emptied the little saloon set within the small town of Silver Springs. It was the look of a man who had but one thing carved into his heartless soul. He wanted the reward money upon his opponent's head. A mere 2,000 American dollars was no great prize in these parts but big enough to bring the dregs of humanity in search of the bandit known simply as Zococa.

The bandit leaned against the bar and toyed with his small thimble-glass filled with tequila. The bottle beside his right elbow still contained the small worm favoured in his native Mexico.

'We know each other, my ugly one?' Zococa asked the reflection in the long greasy mirror set into the wall behind a score of bottle and glasses of various sizes.

'They call me Jake Rochester, Zococa,' said the bounty hunter as he pushed his coat-tails over the grips of his matched

Remingtons. 'I guess you've heard tell of me even down in Mexico.'

Zococa sipped at his drink as he studied the man who moved easily behind him.

'I am sorry to say this but I have not heard of you, *señor*. Are you a bounty hunter?'

The man seemed angered by the smiling reply.

'Turn around and I'll show you who and what I am.'

'I think this is a bad day for you, Jake Rochester.' Zococa placed the empty glass down upon the damp bar-top and eased himself around slowly until he was facing the professional killer.

'I have hunted your sort before. You all die the same way.'

Zococa stared around the saloon which was now empty of anyone apart from themselves. He carefully flicked the leather safety-loop off his silver-plated pistol. His smile still as wide as ever, he took one step away from the bar and lowered his chin as he focused like an eagle upon the mercenary before him.

'You gone a tad quiet, Zococa. You scared?' Rochester spat across the distance between them angrily.

'I must tell the truth, *amigo*. I am never

scared.' Zococa stretched the fingers of his left hand above the gun grip of his solitary holster.

'When a dude smiles the way you smile, I figure he's damn wetting himself, sonny.' Jake Rochester rotated his head as he spoke, as if loosening up his neck muscles for the vicious duel ahead.

Zococa narrowed his eyes and raised his right hand to waist-level as if priming himself for the inevitable fanning of his pistol.

'You lost for words, Zococa?' Rochester snarled.

'I think you do not know much about the great Zococa, *señor*.' The bandit watched the man before readying himself for the inevitable showdown.

'What's to know?' The question was spat out at the bandit in a mixture of chewing-tobacco and spittle.

Zococa grinned. 'I do not ride alone, *señor*.'

For the first time since the bounty hunter had shown his hand and scared away everyone inside the saloon, his face went pale as he absorbed the words.

'There ain't no mention of a gang on your poster, sonny.'

'I do not require the gang, *amigo*. I have a friend though. A very big friend who is standing at the saloon doors with his pistol aimed straight at you.' Zococa raised his eyebrows.

'If you had a partner, how come he weren't in here with you drinking, you Mexican bastard?' Rochester had to use every ounce of his self-discipline to stop himself looking at the saloon doors behind him.

'My friend is Tahoka. He is an Apache warrior and the Americans do not like Indians coming into saloons.' Zococa watched Rochester's hands as they moved closer to the grips of his weapons.

'Am I supposed to believe that?'

The sound of Tahoka's gun hammer being cocked echoed around the saloon. Rochester suddenly felt sweat running down his face from beneath his hatband.

'You're a back-shooter, Zococa,' the bounty hunter snarled as he glanced over at the stony-faced Indian aiming his pistol at him.

Zococa took another step forward. 'Lower your gun, my little rhinoceros,' he ordered the silent Apache.

Tahoka reluctantly did as he was instructed.

16

'This some kinda trick?' Jake Rochester shouted at the bandit.

'I do not play tricks, *señor*. Now it is up to you. You can ride away and we will not harm you, or you can try to claim the reward money.'

'If I kill you, how do I know your tame Apache won't shoot me in the back, Zococa?' the man growled.

'You do not, *señor*,' Zococa responded.

There were no more words. The matched Remingtons were drawn and fired with hands trained for speed. Zococa however was faster and continued fanning his pistol until its hammer fell upon spent chambers.

As the gunsmoke cleared, the bounty hunter lay lifeless in the sawdust. Zococa glanced at his mute friend by the saloon doors and shook his head.

Walking out of the small saloon, Zococa said nothing, but he rested a hand upon the shoulder of the large Indian. As he mounted his pinto stallion he emptied the shells from his gun and began loading it again. As with all victories, it tasted bitter.

It was a mere month later and one of those heavily scented evenings when the sun seemed to hang above the canopy of trees for ever, bathing everything in a glowing golden mist. The posse, led by Sheriff Bob Barker, had crossed the border and ridden deep into the Mexican woods trying to catch just half a glimpse of the two men he knew were ahead of them. The trail had seemingly gone dead several times; then they'd heard the loud laughter ahead of them.

It was the taunting laughter of Zococa the bandit who could not resist leading his pursuers around in circles. Barker would, as he had done countless times in the past, chase the elusive bandit and his Indian companion, Tahoka, like a bloodhound trying to corner a pair of invisible racoons.

In all the years Barker had held office he had never managed to get close to the two men. Somehow, they always managed to stay one jump ahead of him. There were no photographic images of Zococa on his numerous wanted posters; just line-drawings which owed everything to the imagination of the illustrators and nothing to reality. Barker began to wonder if he might have already met the bandit and not recognized him. Only the laughter which rang out amid the trees seemed consistent. That was always the same.

The posse of bedraggled riders drove their lathered mounts into the shallow river and reined in as they reached the middle of the slow-flowing waters. Barker removed his Stetson and sat atop of his old grey, trying to catch his second wind. The rest of his posse were as bewildered as the sheriff.

'Where in tarnation is he, Bob?' one of the older deputies asked as their horses began drinking the cool water.

'He's crossed back into Texas, boys. That's one thing I'm sure of,' Barker snapped, replacing his hat onto his sweating head.

'How many times tonight has he done that, Sheriff?' another voice asked.

'We've been back and forth over this damn river three times in each direction, Sheriff,' yet another man moaned as their horses snorted beneath their saddles.

'Shut up,' Barker ordered as he stared out across the river at the trees and brush before them.

'He's playing with us, Bob,' a tired voice said to Barker's right.

'Again,' another voice agreed.

'I said shut up. I meant it,' Barker growled as he looked at each of his men in turn.

'If we caught the critter, he'd probably steal our guns,' a laughing voice remarked from over the shoulder of the sheriff.

'Come on. We're heading home. I've had enough,' Bob Barker said, shaking his head in defeat. He spurred his grey onwards through the water until they reached the dry ground which led towards the sprawling town set amid a dozen ranches of varying sizes.

As the discouraged members of the posse rode off in their various directions and Barker aimed his horse at the distant town of Rio Concho, the bushes that had been behind them began to rustle. The two riders moved their mounts out into the dying embers of the sun.

'See? I told you they would get tired and go away, my little hippopotamus,' Zococa said as he ran a fine black cigar under his well-educated nostrils, and steadied his large pinto stallion.

The massive Apache shrugged and gazed around them as he moved his flame-faced black gelding alongside the pinto.

'Quiet, Tahoka. You are giving me a headache,' said Zococa. He struck a match across the top of his ornate saddle horn and smiled at his mute friend.

The face of the Indian was as blank as usual as he stared at the grinning bandit who was puffing away at the long cigar. Making a hand signal which caught Zococa's eye, Tahoka pointed at the smoke gripped between his partner's perfect teeth.

'You want a cigar, my little one?' Zococa asked as he pushed his black sombrero off his face.

Tahoka nodded.

'But it will stunt your growth. It will make your muscles weak and flabby. Do you wish that I, the great Zococa, should harm his only true friend by giving him a cigar?' The bandit raised an eyebrow as he watched his friend.

Tahoka nodded again and grunted.

'Very well, but if you get even the slightest bit ill, I shall not help you, Tahoka.' Zococa handed over a cigar and watched as his companion placed it in his mouth and waited.

'I am sorry, *pequeño*. Do you wish a light?'

Tahoka sighed heavily as he watched the smiling man strike another match and hand it to him.

'I think we should ride into Rio Concho and see if there is anyone who wishes to employ the great Zococa.' The bandit gathered up his reins and began riding slowly toward the distant town as his friend followed. Glancing over his shoulder, the bandit grinned at the sight of Tahoka puffing frantically as he spoke with his hands.

Zococa gripped his own cigar between his sparkling teeth.

'Be quiet, my friend. You will wake up the good citizens of Rio Concho with all your babbling and smoke signals.'

The large Indian drew his mount level and gave Zococa a hard look. He knew the Mexican could read his mind as easily as he could read even the faintest of trails.

'Do not frown, my handsome one. I have told you the women hate men with wrinkles.'

The Apache brave waved a hand beside the face of his companion frantically.

'Do not interrupt, Tahoka. I have told you many times it is most rude to keep interrupting the magnificent Zococa when he is trying to get a word in. You seem to think I have nothing better to do than listen to all your endless rantings.'

The Indian looked ahead at the trail which was beginning to disappear as night finally took command. He knew the riders who had chased them were not far ahead of them but also knew it mattered little to his friend.

'Quiet, *amigo*. I know exactly what you are

trying to say. Rio Concho is a very nice town, is it not? The sheriff is a very nice man, is he not? Why do you get so worried on such a beautiful evening as this? I am hungry and you are also hungry and we require funds. Are there not many wealthy men in Rio Concho who will pay us lots of money to do their bidding and thus enable us to eat and drink our fill?'

Tahoka began nodding, sucking feverishly upon his cigar as he rode alongside the smiling bandit.

Zococa laughed. 'I do not know how you do it, my friend, but you have once again persuaded me against my better judgement to visit this town you have been so annoyingly talking about. I just hope there are some pretty ladies there.'

Tahoka shook his head and simply rode his gelding alongside the powerful pinto. The smiling bandit was determined not to allow anything or anyone to spoil his fun. They were going to Rio Concho, it was as simple as that.

TWO

The town of Rio Concho had always felt far more Mexican than Texan to the bandit, who steered his pinto through the shadows with his faithful friend trailing a few yards behind. Its streets rang out with the haunting melodies of Zococa's home far to the south of the border. The sound of countless guitars and trumpets drifted on the warm evening air from dozens of cantinas dotted along the small narrow streets.

It seemed strange to Zococa, as he studied the illuminated store-fronts, that this place could possibly be a gringo town. It was large and seemed to have no true pattern to it like most Texan towns. This was a place that could not conceal its true origins. Streets seemed to wind aimlessly, with edifices of various shapes and sizes placed wherever the builders' fancies had taken them. Only the flags hanging from poles outside the general store and the bank, each with its solitary star sewn into its fabric, belied the illusion that this was anywhere but Texas.

Nevertheless, Zococa liked this town. It had a thousand corners and twice as many shadows, which he could use to evade the knowing eyes of those whom he did not wish to observe his regular visits. His Latin friends, who were still the majority of Rio Concho's citizens, greeted him in silent admiration as his black-and-white horse paced through the maze of alleyways. To them he was a hero, a man who had an almost mythic quality about his wide shoulders. None of these tanned faces would ever betray the famous Zococa.

The perfume of a hundred flowers filled his inflated chest as he drew his horse to a halt outside a small familiar cantina.

Waiting for Tahoka to bring his black gelding up alongside, the bandit glanced around before dismounting. The street torches were few and gave the night a sense of security that Zococa liked.

The Indian threw his long leg over the horse's neck and slid from his saddle silently as he watched the Mexican tying both their reins to the long rickety hitching rail. Silently, Tahoka moved to the side of his smiling friend as they stood in the light of a dozen paper lanterns.

'Hungry?' Zococa asked with a smile as he

cast another indicative glance around the narrow alley that was filled with the sounds and smells he savoured.

Tahoka nodded and followed the smaller, more agile man through the beaded drapes into the cantina. The smell of cooking chilli filled the nostrils of them both.

'I have enough for us to have a quick meal and a bottle of the most inexpensive wine, I think.' Zococa pulled out a silver dollar and showed it to his partner as they seated themselves in a corner at a round table. Placed in the centre of the table a candle burned until the bandit extinguished its flame with his thumb and index finger.

'I do not like candles, *pequeño*. They attract moths and sometimes bullets from misguided heroes.' Zococa removed his sombrero and hung it over the back of his hard chair as he eyed the beautiful female who moved towards them. She was no more than eighteen and probably far younger. Her heavily tanned face made her eyes and teeth appear to sparkle as she greeted the two men she had known for most of her life.

'It is an honour to have you back in my mother's cantina, Zococa,' she said softly, leaning over the table and staring deeply into the bandit's eyes while he stared into her blouse.

Zococa touched the ends of her long black hair and brought them to his lips.

'You are the most beautiful woman I have ever set eyes upon, Conchita. I bathe in your radiance.'

She touched his cheek and traced her long slim finger to his well-trimmed moustache.

'When will you make love to me? I have waited so very long for you to take me to paradise.'

Zococa glanced at his yawning friend before returning his attention to the lovely Conchita. Her low-cut white cotton blouse revealed her firm dark heaving breasts to his willing eyes as he licked his lips.

'I am very busy at the moment, my sweet one. Maybe a little later we could perhaps paddle in the waters of your charms?'

Grabbing his head, Conchita pulled his face into her soft bosom. There was no resistance. Zococa inhaled the heavenly fragrance which drifted from her moist cleavage as he stared down at her dark erect young nipples.

Reluctantly freeing himself, Zococa gripped her hair and gently drew her head down towards his own until his lips found hers. Only when he had kissed her for a good five minutes did he release her. Gasping for air Conchita leaned against the wall above the two men as if her body had been drained of every ounce of its strength.

'Perhaps later we shall visit heaven together?' Zococa smiled.

Conchita nodded as she walked breathlessly back to the cooking area still gasping for air.

Tahoka tapped his partner's shoulder and pointed to his mouth and then his belly.

'I know you are hungry. She will bring us some food when she has fully recovered.' Zococa pulled out a long silver case from his inside jacket pocket and opened it to reveal a half dozen slim black cigars. Offering one to the bored Apache brave he put one in his own mouth.

'You see how hard it is for me? Everywhere I go these ravishing females throw themselves at me. What am I to do? I cannot insult them by ignoring their pleas for my attention, can I?'

Tahoka leaned forward and accepted the light from Zococa's match. He inhaled the strong smoke as he watched the grinning Mexican puffing on his own cigar.

'It is so unfair, Tahoka. There are so many women and only one Zococa. Is this not cruel? I have to try to ration myself out so each one of them has a little pleasure in their otherwise boring lives.'

The Indian watched as an older woman came towards them with a tray containing two bowls of chilli and large chunks of freshly baked bread. Placing it down upon the table, she began smiling at the bandit knowingly.

'You are so wicked, Zococa,' the female sighed.

'Can a fox help but be attracted to juicy chickens, lovely lady?' He watched as the older woman removed the dishes from her tray and placed them before Tahoka and himself.

'A bottle of wine, Zococa?'

'*Si,* my beautiful one.' The bandit watched as the giggling woman picked up the silver dollar and slid it between her more than ample breasts. Straightening up, she gave him a quick pinch on his cheek and then returned to the cooking area of the aromatic cantina.

'Conchita's mother is very nice also. A little wide but still young enough to...' Zococa's words faded as he caught the disapproving stare of his friend, who sat holding a cigar in one hand and a spoon in the other. Shrugging, the bandit started to stir his spoon around in the bowl of rich chilli as he began thinking of their situation. They had been down on their luck many times over the years but never totally without funds as they were now. As Zococa watched his friend consuming the meal which he knew would go nowhere near filling his large frame, he decided to ignore his own hunger. Pushing his own bowl of chilli across the table, he nodded.

'I do not have the appetite to eat at the moment, *amigo*. Finish this for me?'

Tahoka raised an eyebrow and stared at this partner for a few seconds before pulling the bowl in front of him. The Mexican smiled and then also slid the bread across the table towards his friend.

The still blushing Conchita returned and placed the opened bottle of wine on their table. She flashed her eyes at Zococa who nodded as she walked away. Her hips swayed back and forth like the pendulum of a large clock.

Zococa poured a glass of wine into his glass, leaned back and tried to think of a way to replenish their fortunes before the sun rose once again. As he sipped at the dark red wine his eyes began to twinkle.

THREE

Zococa and his faithful companion Tahoka
had only just mounted their horses outside
the cantina when a small bare-foot boy
dressed entirely in white came rushing
towards them. The bandit pulled his reins
up to his chin as he watched the child
staring up at him in awe. Zococa had
witnessed such admiration many times but
he still relished it.

'Be careful, little one. An open mouth can
be visited by a hundred moths.' Zococa
smiled as he pulled his sombrero off his
back and put it on his head again.

'Are you the great Zococa, *señor*?' the boy
asked.

'*Sí*. I am the great Zococa, little one.
Why?' The bandit leaned down and stared
into the face of the boy who seemed nervous
and unsure.

'A man asked me to give you this letter.'
The boy gave the note to the curious bandit.

Zococa opened the scrap of paper and
studied it carefully for a few moments

before noticing that the child was still standing beside his left stirrup-guard with his hand outstretched.

'Thank you, my brave one,' Zococa said to the boy.

'The man said you would give me a silver dollar for bringing this message to you, Zococa,' the boy said, still holding out his small grubby hand.

The bandit glanced across at Tahoka before shrugging as he returned his attention to the child.

'I do not have a silver dollar on me at the moment, by bold friend,' Zococa began. 'I do have this though.'

The boy watched as the famous bandit pulled out a bullet from his gun-belt and handed it down to the child.

'This is just a bullet, *señor*. I do not understand,' the boy said, looking at the cartridge.

'It's not just a bullet. It is one of the great Zococa's bullets. Bring it back to me tomorrow and I shall give you two silver dollars for it.' Zococa watched as the boy's face began to beam with a smile and he ran off happily into the night.

Tahoka used his hands to ask Zococa what was in the note that the boy had brought.

'This is money, *amigo*.' Zococa grinned as

he turned his pinto stallion away from the cantina and spurred it on down the dark alley. The Indian steered his flame-faced black gelding after his whistling friend. As he drew level, Zococa held the paper up and kissed it.

'I have always said that there is an evil man in every town and it is our job to find him, Tahoka. It seems this evil man knew we were in Rio Concho and wants to meet with us.'

Tahoka made a confused face.

'This note gives an address in the better part of town and the writer wishes to meet with the brave Zococa to discuss something which will be of mutual benefit,' said the Mexican as he teased his reins, gently guiding the large horse through the maze of buildings.

The Apache nodded knowingly as he aimed his horse after the pinto. He knew Zococa would never willingly do anything which might harm innocent people, but he would take the money and create havoc, given half a chance. If the smiling bandit had one thing he did extremely well, it was in his ability to confuse even the most intelligent of opponents. It was a game he played with such skill that no living man had ever managed to better him.

The house was only just in the better part of Rio Concho and Zococa noticed this immediately as he stepped from his saddle and tied his reins to a large bush. Tahoka slid from the saddle and wrapped his own reins around his partner's saddle horn before silently moving to his side. Zococa was studying the note carefully.

'This is the address, I think.'

The stony-faced Indian agreed and walked beside his partner as they made their way up through the avenue of fruit-trees towards the large building.

'It is not as nice a house as the ones further down the street, Tahoka,' Zococa observed as he moved to the large black door and tapped upon it with the barrel of his silver-plated pistol.

There was a long silence before the door eventually opened to reveal a frail man in a uniform which was designed to keep him in his proper place for the duration of his pitiful existence.

'You must be Zococa,' the retainer uttered in a tone which denoted distaste.

'*Si*, my stiff one. I am the legendary Zococa. Who are you?'

'I am Bates, sir. I am merely the butler,'

the man said as he ushered them into the dimly illuminated hall of the house before closing the door behind them.

'Do not put yourself down, Bates. I am sure you are a very good butler. Whatever a butler is.' The bandit held onto his pistol as the man led them through several dark rooms until they reached a place which glowed in comparison, revealing a figure leaning against a marble pillar.

He was big by normal standards yet Tahoka was taller than the man in the red silk smoking-jacket. He said nothing as Bates waved the two trail-weary men into the large room.

'You sent me this note, *señor*?' Zococa asked, waving the scrap of paper under the man's nose. He circled the tall figure, taking careful note of every detail of his appearance.

'You are Zococa?' The man's voice sounded different from any other the bandit had ever heard. It had an accent which Zococa could not place.

'I am the great Zococa, my friend. Who, might I be so bold as to ask, are you?'

'My name is unimportant. I'm hiring you to do a job,' the man said as he moved to a handsome chair and seated himself down to watch his guests.

The bandit twirled his gun as he paced around the room taking note of all the obvious symbols of wealth. The fine books in an even finer bookcase. A grand table which looked as if it had taken an entire tree in its construction. Silver and gold ornaments were dotted everywhere and a decorative china service reposed upon the three-leaf highly polished table. This man certainly had a lot of money and it seemed a reasonable guess that he had not acquired these things honestly, otherwise he would never have sent for Zococa.

'Your name, *señor*?' the smiling bandit asked once more.

'My name is Jason O'Hara,' their host reluctantly announced in a voice which seemed to have lost half its volume.

Tahoka touched his partner's sleeve and eyed the man's right hand which was buried deep within the pocket of his smoking-jacket.

'You noticed it as well, my friend. Well done.' Zococa grinned broadly.

'What are you talking about to that damned redskin?' O'Hara snapped at the Mexican.

Zococa frowned briefly before resuming

his natural smiling ways as he slowly walked up to the seated figure. Aiming his pistol at O'Hara's head he began speaking in a quiet controlled fashion as if afraid he might lose control of his emotions.

'Firstly, my friend here is not a redskin. He is a warrior of the Apache nation. Secondly, he, like myself, noticed that you have a small-barrelled gun concealed in your right hand which makes me very angry. Please remove your hand from your pocket very slowly or I shall be forced to dissolve our partnership before it has even begun.'

Knowing his guest was not bluffing, Jason O'Hara withdrew his hand from the pocket of his smoking-jacket with the gun hanging limply on his index finger. Zococa took the pistol and tossed it to Tahoka who emptied its shells onto the table before throwing it back into the hands of the trembling O'Hara. Only then did Zococa holster his weapon and sit on the arm of a chair opposite his now sweating host.

'What is this job you wish me to consider?' Zococa asked.

O'Hara gave a huge sigh before saying, 'You're as good as they say you are, Zococa.'

'This I already know. What is the job you wish me to undertake on your behalf?'

Zococa leaned forward and stared directly into O'Hara's eyes.

'They say you are a hired gun. Is this true?' O'Hara asked drily.

'I am the greatest gunman in the world, *señor*. Continue.'

'I require someone eliminated.' The statement was brief and somewhat cryptic.

Zococa glanced at his friend briefly as he thought about the four little words.

'Am I correct in thinking you wish my services to end someone's life, O'Hara?'

Jason O'Hara swallowed before nodding.

'How much are you willing to pay the great Zococa to do this thing, Jason O'Hara?'

'A thousand dollars. Hard cash.'

'This is a nice round figure.' Zococa touched his moustache with his long trigger finger as he thought about Conchita back at the cantina and her even better figure.

'Is it a deal?'

'Not so fast, my sweating one.' Zococa waved his hands in the air as he weighed up the proposition.

'I'll pay you fifty per cent up front and the rest when you've done the job.'

Zococa began to think about the man opposite him. Who exactly was this Jason

O'Hara? Who was the intended victim? Nothing O'Hara had said seemed to make a great deal of sense, yet he was in dire need of funds, and this total stranger was willing to pay him hard cash. It was an opportunity too rare to resist.

'I think I will do this job.' Zococa smiled.

O'Hara seemed to relax. He watched the man in the sombrero as he walked around the large room deep in thought.

'You agree to my terms?'

Zococa paused as he reached a large silver box upon a small table; curious, he opened it. His eyes widened as he saw the expensive cigars lined up inside its blue satin interior, like little brown troopers. Scooping up a handful, Zococa walked to Tahoka's side and gave all but one to the huge Apache.

'First I wish to have the name of the victim, *señor*.'

'He's called Frank Wilson. He has a small spread due west of Rio Concho,' O'Hara said quickly as he watched Zococa striking a match and lighting his and his partner's cigars in turn.

'Then I think we have a deal, *señor* O'Hara. I would like my five hundred dollars now, if you please.' Zococa puffed on the mild cigar as he eyed O'Hara, who rose from his chair and walked across to a small desk.

Looking over his shoulder, O'Hara spoke.

'I imagine you would like it in small-denomination bills, Zococa?'

'Very thoughtful.' Zococa smiled as he watched O'Hara bring the bundle of notes across the room. He handed it over.

Pushing the money into his inside jacket pocket, Zococa turned to leave the room, followed by Tahoka.

'You aren't going to count it, Zococa?' O'Hara asked as the pair reached the doorway.

'I trust you, *señor*.' The bandit smiled as he bowed his farewell.

Music was filling the streets as Zococa and Tahoka led their horses through the scented alley deeper into the better part of Rio Concho. The houses were larger here, set away from the streets in large well-maintained gardens behind tall walls. These were dwellings far older than the town itself and echoed a time long since gone when this place lay beneath a different flag.

'I know what you are going to say, my friend. You are going to ask why I, the bold Zococa, agreed to kill this man called Frank

Wilson when he has done nothing to harm you or me. Am I correct?' Zococa stared at Tahoka's emotionless face. It was solid, like a carved wooden mask. Only the eyes moved as they flashed that very question to him.

'Do you think I would really kill for a mere thousand dollars, Tahoka?' Zococa asked, pausing at a tall iron gate set between eight-foot-tall stone pillars anchored to a solid boundary wall.

The Indian grunted and shook his head as he looked about them nervously.

'I think we must go visit this Frank Wilson, though,' Zococa said thoughtfully. 'I am curious as to what sort of person he is to be so hated by Jason O'Hara.'

Tahoka patted the Mexican on his back before noticing how interested he seemed to be in the elegant house set in the well-sculptured gardens. The Indian grunted and waved a finger under the nose of his partner.

'Do not worry. I am not going to steal anything from these good people. Even though they probably have so much that they might not even notice. No, I am just admiring the beautiful lines of the building. Is it not elegant?'

Tahoka shrugged.

'Buildings such as these were built by artists such as myself, not gringos who have no flair for beauty.' Zococa sighed as he fondly patted the thick bundle of five-dollar bills in his jacket pocket. He could still see the face of Jason O'Hara in his mind's eye as he leaned against the iron gates. It was an image of which he knew it was wise to be wary.

Zococa suddenly saw a figure within the garden moving around beneath hanging lanterns.

Tapping the Apache, Zococa pointed to a young woman who seemed to float amongst the trees and cascades of flowers. She was blonde and young and she was crying.

'She is sobbing, my friend. How can such a lovely creature be so unhappy?'

Tahoka gripped the bars of the tall gate and stared in at the haunting figure of the young woman who was indeed crying as she moved around the vast garden, which was bathed in shadows, and made her way to a large ornamental pool set beneath a great tree. Tahoka turned to his partner, just in time to catch sight of Zococa's high heels as they disappeared over the wall.

FOUR

Zococa moved like a mountain cat through the large branches of the ancient tree. The thick broad leaves would have given him perfect cover in the daylight, and here, during the hours of haunting darkness, he moved unseen until he was directly above the large circular pool. Zococa paused for a few moments, gazing down at the sobbing figure bathed in the blue haze of nightfall before carefully laying himself across the broad branches. Using his long artistic fingers silently to part the leaves in front of his face, the bandit lowered his head until he could see her clearly. Her face seemed radiant as it reflected in the smooth dark waters of the pool. From his vantage point, he could see the tears rolling down her face. If anything touched the soul of Zococa, it was the crying of a female.

The attractive young blonde sat upon the low wall which surrounded the ornamental pond. Her eyes, wet with tears, stared blankly into the water as it reflected the branches of the great tree that reached out above her. The light from the string of hanging lanterns barely touched this part of the beautifully kept garden and she felt secure here. Then, as her moist eyes began to focus upon the dark water within the pool, she began to see something which, although surprising, did not create one tremor of worry within her. It was the face of Zococa, reflecting a concerned expression.

For a brief moment, she felt as if she were a small girl once more looking for mystical beings in the magical waters.

'Do not cry, my little one,' Zococa whispered down at the young woman.

'Who are you? Are you real, or am I dreaming?' her voice whispered to the reflection.

'I am very real, my golden-haired beauty,' replied the gentle voice.

'I must be dreaming.' The young woman covered her face with her small hands as if afraid that she was beginning to lose her mind.

'Do not be distressed, my lovely one. I am a mere man who was drawn to your weeping. I am above you in the branches of your stout tree.' Zococa gave another smile as he watched her slowly straightening up.

His words seemed to soothe her. Cautiously, she turned and looked upward into the dense foliage until she saw the smiling face of Zococa looking down.

'Who are you, stranger?'

'I am a worthless creature who is ashamed to have deceived you for even the briefest of moments, dear lady.'

'You must have a name. What is it?'

Their eyes locked and it was as if they had known each other's souls for a hundred lifetimes.

'They call me Zococa.' His grin seemed to grow even wider.

Her face suddenly brightened as she responded to the name he had feared might frighten her.

'Zococa the bandit?'

'*Sì.* I am the great Zococa.'

'Why are you up in that tree?'

'This, I do not usually do.' Zococa grinned and lowered himself down to the ground beside her.

'You heard me crying and came to offer a gentle word of compassion, Zococa?' Her beauty was unmatched by any he had seen in his entire life. Her skin was pale and delicate, as if it had never been exposed to the vicious rays of the Texas sun. Her hair was like the purest spun gold. Even in the half-light of night-time, Zococa could see her eyes were a pale blue or grey. She was unlike any other female he had ever met and he had known many.

'I am pleased you have ceased crying,' the bandit said softly, noticing her eyes beginning to dry as they studied him.

'It's strange. Suddenly I don't seem to feel so unhappy, Zococa.' Her words were soft, like her captivating features, as they poured over him.

'Why were you crying on such a beautiful evening?' he asked as he tried to resist the urge to take her in his arms and kiss her. Zococa seldom met any female without falling in love, even if it were for only a matter of a few minutes. Keeping his hands off such a divine creature took every scrap of his self-control.

'It is a sadness that is my own,' she said woefully.

Zococa walked slowly around her small slender body, staring at her closely. She was so tiny compared to the usual women he encountered. Then, as he moved to a spot where the low moon was directly behind her, it seemed as if he could see right through her dress. Zococa stood resting his chin on his knuckles as he enjoyed the sight. It was a feast for his tired eyes but worthy of every second he wasted upon it.

'Let me be the judge of whether your troubles are also my troubles, my fair one.'

She looked at him with an expression of surprise etched into her luminous features.

'Why would you want to help me? You do not even know me, Zococa.'

Moving his head to one side, the bandit drank in the vision of her almost transparent dress.

'I see you are a beautiful young woman. You have no secrets from the legendary Zococa. I see everything.'

'I had heard you were the bravest of men but I had no idea how true that statement was, until now.' She sighed.

'Explain to me everything and if it is possible, I will help you.' Zococa tried to take his eyes off the radiant form but it was impossible.

'It is a long story.'

'I have much time.'

'Then I shall tell you everything, great Zococa.'

Zococa stepped closer to her. 'Before you do, please tell me what is your name, my golden one?'

'My name is Elizabeth Woodrow,' came her reply.

The bandit nodded. 'That is a very hard name for one such as I to remember.'

Elizabeth Woodrow stepped closer to him and touched his cheek tenderly with the palm of her tiny hand. Zococa took hold of it and brought it to his lips.

'Then call me Beth.'

Zococa smiled as he released her hand.

'Beth is a name I can remember quite easily.'

Tahoka had waited for the better part of an hour for his partner to reappear over the high boundary wall. He had mounted his flame-faced black gelding when his feet had started to ache and had soon dozed off as he leaned against the gate pillars. The sound of Zococa dropping from the tree and landing in his saddle beside Tahoka brought the Apache out of his deep slumbers.

'Do not be frightened, my gentle rhinoceros,' Zococa said patting his friend upon his firm muscular shoulder as he took in a deep breath.

Rubbing his sore eyes, Tahoka nodded at his partner as he talked with his nimble fingers and hands. Question after question fluttered towards the smiling Mexican.

'What was I doing, you ask?' Zococa tilted his head and smiled broadly.

Tahoka grunted as he searched for his own reins amid the mane of the black horse.

'I met the most beautiful female in all of Rio Concho, my little one. She like Zococa.'

The Apache raised his eyebrows and shook his head as if he knew what must have occurred between his partner and the blonde female.

'It is not what you think, brave one. She was very sad and I made her exceedingly happy because I said we would try very hard to help her.'

Tahoka raised both his arms as if pleading with his gods for help. How many times since they had been together had the big-hearted bandit risked everything because of a beautiful face?

'I did not make love to her, if that is what you are thinking, Tahoka. I am a gentleman and never take advantage of lovely ladies. She explained everything to me and do you know what? It is very strange. She is in love with a man called Frank Wilson who has a small rancho...' Zococa watched as his partner turned and stared straight at him with renewed interest.

'Frank Wilson! You know, the man we said we would kill for the rich gringo, Jason O'Hara. Is this not a very odd thing, my little one?'

Tahoka held his reins firmly in his strong hands as he watched his friend pulling his sombrero up from his back and placing it on his head.

'The little golden-haired female named Beth has told me a lot of things. Things which are very interesting because it seems our dark-hearted *Señor* O'Hara is even more wicked than I first thought. It would appear that O'Hara is also even richer than I originally thought but this wealth has twisted him. He thinks money can buy him anything he wants. And I think you probably know what he wants.'

Tahoka pointed through the gates and then made a gesture which meant 'girl'.

'*Sì*, my little elephant.' Zococa pulled his horse away from the wall.

The two riders spurred their mounts into action. The pinto stallion led the way through the dimly illuminated streets of Rio Concho until they had negotiated all its twists and turns and finally found themselves out in the fertile countryside. With the smell of fruit-trees drifting on the night air, both Zococa and Tahoka rode for the small ranch owned by the man they only knew as Frank Wilson.

FIVE

Twenty-four-year-old Frank Wilson was already awake and hard at work when dawn finally arrived. The heat from the blistering sun seemed immediately to transform the ranch as its fire engulfed everything it touched. A solitary rooster stood upon the tin roof of the hen-house, proclaiming to all who could hear that a new day was beginning. The small ranch was nothing by Texan standards but it was well maintained and self-sufficient. A few milk-cows in one of its three main pastures provided sufficient dairy products for Wilson and there was always enough left over to sell in nearby Rio Concho. An orchard of mature apple-trees filled the surrounding area with the aroma of fruit whilst a small garden to the side of the wooden house never failed to supply the young rancher with fresh vegetables, as a windmill drew water up from the ground in plentiful quantities. There was only one black spot on this idyllic landscape and that was the lower pasture, which lay a quarter of a mile away from Wilson's house. The young rancher had vainly tried to make the boggy land along this thirty-acre strip as productive as the rest of his property. Nothing that his meagre resources could afford had worked. The land was more swamp than pasture and gave off a worse odour than a hundred privies as it belched up gas and black tar.

Frank Wilson was no quitter but even he knew when a cause was lost and had reluctantly fenced off the offending pasture. It had meant losing a sixth of his land, but at least he would not lose his small herd.

With careful management, this was a place where a man with or without a family could live quite handsomely provided money was not his overriding goal. The young man had proved he had what it took to make this place work and yet the reason for all his backbreaking toil was still many miles away, living like a prisoner with her rich father.

Elizabeth 'Beth' Woodrow had not reached the age when she was entitled to make her own decisions and Wilson knew it was doubtful that she ever would. She was like a priceless gem in these parts and valuable to a father who placed monetary significances upon everything, including his only child.

The young hardworking man had seen how Jacob Woodrow had changed when he had first noticed that Beth had started to blossom. Wilson knew Woodrow had fallen on hard times because of his greed and bad business deals, and that he was planning to marry his daughter off to the highest bidder.

For a man like Jacob Woodrow who had once prided himself on owning dozens of slaves, this was merely another step into his own personal cesspit.

Frank Wilson had just collected a dozen fresh eggs from his hen-house and was making his way across the courtyard towards his house when he noticed his old hound-dog staring up towards the tree-filled hills. Stopping for a second, the young man gazed up at what had caught the dog's attention.

Then he saw them.

For a moment he tried to dismiss the two riders who sat watching him from their high vantage-point, but as he reached the porch of his house, sweat began flowing down his spine, soaking the tail of his shirt. The old hound-dog which trailed his every step suddenly sat down and began wagging its tail at the sight of the two riders.

'Some guard dog you are, Crow,' Wilson exhaled.

He placed the basket of eggs down on his porch chair; then he leaned over and picked up his rusting old shotgun which was propped against the wall, before walking back to the side of the strangely quiet dog.

He checked that the weapon was loaded, then stood over the hound and lifted a hand to shield his eyes.

'You're supposed to bark, you flea-bag!'

The dog lay down and panted as its master bit his lower lip nervously.

'Ain't normal for visitors to call this early,' Wilson mumbled to himself and his dog as he stood trying to make out the two riders. All he knew for certain was that there were two of them.

For a while his eyes were not sure what they were looking at, but as the two horses began to ride down the road towards him he started to focus more clearly. As he realized what he was observing, Wilson began to wish he had stayed close to his house, where there was some cover.

As the pair of riders reached his roughly made gate, Wilson felt sick to the pit of his stomach. To see a man wearing a sombrero was nothing unusual in these parts, but when he rode beside a stony-faced Apache, something was not quite right. When both men were heavily armed as these were, a rusting old single-shot shotgun just did not seem to be a suitable deterrent.

'Hold up,' Frank Wilson called out. The two riders reined in their mounts.

'You must be the man we seek.' Zococa smiled from atop his pinto stallion.

Using every ounce of his courage, the young man began edging forward with his ancient rifle in his hands. The dog seemed neither worried nor concerned by either of the visitors and remained upon the ground bathing in the morning sunlight.

'I don't cotton to no trouble, boys,' Wilson said drily as he watched the two men.

'You are called Frank Wilson, *señor*?' Zococa asked, removing his sombrero and dabbing his brow with his sleeve.

Wilson stopped in his tracks.

'You know my name?'

Zococa glanced at Tahoka briefly before returning his attention to the healthy-looking rancher.

'*Sí*. We know of your name but we have the little problem which we would like to discuss with you.'

'What kinda problem?' Wilson looked hard up at the Mexican bandit.

'We have been sent by two different people

on two very different missions. One is nice but the other is not so nice, my friend.' Zococa placed his large black sombrero back on his head.

'I'm getting a tad anxious, mister,' Wilson said down the length of his rifle barrel.

'I am also getting a little anxious. You have a very old rifle in your hands and it has been my experience that such weapons have an annoying habit of shooting people. Even when their trigger has not been squeezed. Would you mind lowering the shotgun?' Zococa liked what he saw in this young man but did not like the look of the rusting rifle.

'How do I know you ain't bandits?' Wilson asked, still aiming the rifle in their direction.

Zococa looked at his partner who shrugged.

'I did not say we were not bandits, Frank Wilson. I am the famous Zococa and this is my trusty friend Tahoka. We do not mean you harm, though.'

Wilson's jaw dropped. 'You *are* bandits. I've heard of you, Zococa.'

'*Sì, señor*. I am famous.' Zococa grinned.

'You've been sent to kill me, ain't you?' Frank Wilson's face had lost its healthy glow as he stared wide-eyed at the smiling rider in front of him.

Zococa rubbed his face and looked at his silent partner.

'This is not going the way I wished it to go, Tahoka.'

'How come your pal don't talk, Zococa?' Wilson tried to hold his gun steady as his hands began shaking.

'Tahoka is without the tongue, Frank Wilson. He is very chatty otherwise, though.'

Frank Wilson began to pace around the two seated riders as he kept the long gun trained upon his uninvited visitors.

'Who sent you here?'

'I told you. Two people. One an evil ruthless rich man and the other an angel with golden hair named Beth.' Zococa watched as the face of Frank Wilson suddenly changed as he heard the name of his sweetheart.

'Beth sent you?'

Zococa nodded.

'Is she OK?' Wilson's agitated concern overwhelmed all his fears for himself.

Zococa shrugged. 'It is hard to say why someone so beautiful has such a heavy heart, but I think she is missing you, my friend.'

The two men dismounted from their horses and Wilson led them towards a full trough of crystal-clear liquid. He lowered his gun as he sat down on the porch, where presently Zococa and Tahoka came to join him in its shade.

'A man such as you should marry his sweetheart and make many babies, I think,' the bandit said. He picked up the rifle and handed it to Tahoka, who removed its single round of ammunition.

'It ain't as easy as that, Zococa.' Wilson sighed.

'It is always easy to get the girl if you have a fast horse, *señor*.' Zococa could see in the young man another person with pain carved into his soul.

'I've only got me an old plough horse, Zococa.' Wilson looked up at the bandit who was straddling the rail of the porch, staring down at the chickens which were beginning their daily ritual of gathering around the house.

Zococa's eyes flashed at the young rancher.

'I have not eaten for a whole day, Frank Wilson. I am very hungry. Tahoka is also very hungry.'

Wilson was thinking about other things as he answered. 'I ain't got much in the larder.'

'But you have chickens. Many fat juicy

chickens.' Zococa drew his silver-plated pistol and twirled it on his trigger finger.

'You want chicken?' Wilson rubbed his temple with his fingers as he watched the skill of his guest with the weapon.

'Fried chicken, I think.' Zococa stopped spinning his gun and fired three times before holstering it.

Frank Wilson waved his hands at the choking gunsmoke before noticing the three dead hens being gathered up by the tall Tahoka.

'I ain't never refused a man a meal, Zococa. But times are hard and I can't afford to lose so many hens in one go.'

The smiling bandit reached into his jacket pocket and peeled off a five-dollar bill which he handed to the young man.

'This will cover it?'

Wilson accepted the five dollars and nodded.

'Tahoka will prepare the birds for our breakfast if you will light your stove.' Zococa watched as the troubled youth stood and took hold of the door handle.

'You said an evil man sent you here, Zococa,' Wilson said quietly.

'*Sí*. A man called Jason O'Hara paid Tahoka and myself to come and kill you,'

Zococa affirmed.

Wilson looked at his empty shotgun resting beside the tall Apache and felt his throat going dry as the gentle hand of the Mexican rested upon his shoulder.

'He sent you to kill me, Zococa?' Frank Wilson's mouth stayed open after he repeated the words which had dropped so effortlessly from the tongue of the confident bandit. His mind raced as he thought about the rich O'Hara paying money to have him killed. Did he fear him so much?

'Is it not amusing?' Zococa smiled.

'That ain't the word I'd have used.'

SIX

It was not Jacob Woodrow's practice to rise before dawn, but the fifty-eight-year-old did so on this dry morning. Sleep, of late, had become something he found taxing. Plagued by thoughts of his own financial downfall, Woodrow had become obsessed by his only remaining asset, his daughter Elizabeth. He knew time was running out if he were to capitalize upon her relative innocence and forestall her increasing interest in the penniless Frank Wilson. How far their relationship had developed, the self-centred man could only speculate. Woodrow had determined long ago to crush any romantic feelings his daughter displayed to anyone as soon as they became apparent.

Beth's happiness just did not have any place in his overall strategy for getting what he wanted. She was still his to do with as he wished.

But it was not this which haunted Jacob Woodrow whenever he tried to seek a few hours' rest at night. Where dreams had once soothed his conscience, now nightmares mocked him. Yet whatever it was that kept eating away at the once wealthy man, it was not anything he could share with another living soul. His was a past filled with ghosts and yet only impending poverty had enabled them to raise their heads and strike out at him.

The face of Woodrow, as he strolled out into his heavily shaded garden, was marked by years of self-indulgence as well as lack of sleep. He looked far older than he actually was, and moved stiffly on feet which burned with every step. Fate had sought repayment for all the years of lavish living. Even the great house had now been heavily mortgaged in a futile attempt to continue the pretence.

His was a tortured life now as all his past misdeeds came back to fill his tired brain. Yet, even these terrifying memories could not stop him from putting his last evil plan into action. There would be only one winner if it succeeded and that winner would be Woodrow himself. Even though he intended to sacrifice his only child's happiness for the right price, Jacob Woodrow did not care.

For him, only his own welfare mattered. He was one of those thankfully rare creatures who, unlike normal men who could look at a flower and see its beauty, asked only its value. What was the potential profit? It had been men such as Woodrow who had destroyed the once endless buffalo herds which roamed the plains like a dark living sea. They would stack the skulls a hundred feet high and feel nothing. Jacob Woodrow had lived his life with similar insouciance.

For the past few months, Woodrow had kept Beth a prisoner within his home. She was allowed in the gardens but only he had a key to the massive gates. Few knew what went on, now or in the past, behind the high walls that guarded his property so well.

Woodrow knew. These were the night-mares which had returned to his desperate mind. All the things which his self-indulgent personality had lavished upon himself for so long were beginning to be remembered. Things which were beyond any normal man's ability to cope with and had been locked away in the dark recesses of a closed mind, had returned.

Beside the crumbling stables beyond the house, hidden from prying eyes, stood the small sod structures where he had once housed his slaves. There had been dozens of slaves over the decades during which he had prospered and each of them female. Woodrow had bought them young and used them as only sick men use chained women. They were cheap flesh and allowed him to travel into a depraved world he would never have dared to enter with his own late wife. One by one he had disposed of them when they no longer roused his interest or when they had become pregnant. Some had made him a handsome profit whilst others had been buried in the dead of night beside the high walls. Exactly how many of these female slaves lay beneath the soil of his garden, only Woodrow knew. Even he had long ago forgotten the total number.

These were his ghosts.

Now it seemed he had become their victim.

Jacob Woodrow sucked feverishly on his cigar as he found himself beside the ornamental pool under the broad branches of the huge tree. He stared down at the soft ground. His face went pale as he noticed two very different sets of footprints. He recognized those of his daughter instantly but the other prints shook his confidence. They were high-heeled-boot prints.

A man had been out here with her the

previous night and had stayed for quite a long time, judging by the way the ground had been cut up, Woodrow mused. Would Frank Wilson have the courage to defy him? Staring angrily up at his daughter's bedroom window he clenched both his fists. What if they had finally consummated their love? Would they dare?

Jacob Woodrow inhaled the acrid smoke of his cigar and tried to think about the situation calmly. There was no call for panic but there was also no time to waste. He knew of Jason O'Hara's interest and had kept the man at arm's length, trying to exploit the situation and increase his daughter's value to the wealthy businessman.

He vowed he would act today. There was no more time to waste if he were to execute his plan. In his fevered brain, Woodrow feared that Frank Wilson had climbed over his garden walls and been with Beth. From now on she would be locked in the house until he had arranged the wedding. The man stormed fuming around the building towards the dilapidated stable where the last of his horses was housed. It would take him at least thirty minutes to harness the pitiful creature to his buggy; time during which he would work out the exact words he would use when he met with the elusive Jason O'Hara. Words which would bleed the best price imaginable from the rich recluse.

SEVEN

Sheriff Bob Barker had been unable to sleep, and found himself walking along the silent streets of Rio Concho just after sunrise. For hours he had roamed the silent alleys looking for anything which might soothe his soul and rid himself of the guilt and embarrassment which burned at his guts.

Once again his futile attempts to capture the notorious bandits had failed and he feared for his reputation. How many times could he rustle a posse together to chase the elusive Zococa before he became a laughing stock? Barker stepped up onto the boardwalk outside his office and searched his pockets for the keys when a chill overwhelmed him. There was no breeze but he had felt as if someone had just stridden across his grave.

Perhaps he was already the butt of everyone's jokes.

'You OK, Bob?'

The sheriff turned towards the friendly familiar voice and touched the brim of his

Stetson. He had known the elegant owner of the Scotsman Saloon, Donna Drumbar for more than a decade and yet this was the first time he could recall her using his first name.

'Miss Drumbar.'

'I heard tell of last evening's charade, Bob.' Her lips were painted and yet still seemed as full and as moist as when he had first encountered them.

'That Zococa ran us around again,' Barker admitted as he tried to fathom her interest. Was she like most of the locals, soft on the smiling bandit, or did she feel sorry for an ageing lawman who had been humiliated once again?

'Men like you should not get themselves worked up over a sly coyote like Zococa, Bob.' She brushed past him and his head suddenly filled with her expensive perfume.

'I'm getting a tad old for chasing shadows, Miss Drumbar,' he said thoughtfully.

For the briefest of moments she paused and her eyes flashed at him.

'My name's Donna, Bob. And you ain't that old.'

'I sure feel it today, Donna,' the sheriff admitted as he watched her swaying hips moving along the boardwalk towards her saloon.

'Call in sometime, Bob. A man like you could use some female company, I reckon.' Her voice seemed to hang on the morning air like the scent of blossoming trees.

'I might just do that,' Bob Barker muttered under his breath as he finally located his office keys and thrust them into the old lock. Twisting his wrist he felt the bolt release.

Stepping into the office he raised the shades and leaned his elbows on the brass rail which fronted the window. Out there a couple of hundred Rio Concho citizens knew of his failure to get even within spitting distance of the great Zococa. Most of those people were Mexican like the bandit himself and Barker knew only too well whom their sympathies lay with. To them it was Zococa who was the hero whilst he was the black-hearted lawman who tried to bring him to justice.

Why did he bother?

What might happen if he did manage the seemingly impossible and capture the laughing Mexican? Who stood more chance of getting hanged?

Bob Barker gulped and ran his fingers over his own throat as he felt the sweat trickling down from under the band of his

Stetson. Zococa wasn't even worth all that much, the sheriff thought. Why did he ever bother to try and capture him?

Pride? Maybe it was the last flickering embers of a fire which had once burned brightly when he had been a younger, more confident sheriff. Now it seemed as if everything took a lot more effort and time. Did he chase Zococa because it was his job or because he wanted to prove something to himself? Whatever the true reasons, Barker knew the laughing bandit simply had a way of getting under his skin. It was a challenge he seemed helpless to ignore and yet he knew in his heart that it was Zococa who was pulling the strings.

Zococa thrilled at being chased by armed men. It was a game.

Then as he rubbed the sweat off his face, Bob Barker saw a dilapidated buggy passing the window of his office.

Barker rubbed his unshaven chin as he wondered why Jacob Woodrow was up so early. Woodrow was a man who seldom ventured out before mid-afternoon on the best of days. The sheriff ran a thumbnail across his teeth until the buggy was no longer in view. For many years he had wondered about Jacob Woodrow and his business dealings and gambling. The man had long ceased to have any visible means of income and yet he still lived the high life. It troubled the sheriff. There had been a hundred rumours about Woodrow but nothing anyone could prove. Barker remembered the tales of the female slaves whom, it was said, the man used for his own carnal gratification. Then there were the stories about the wife who died in mysterious circumstances, leaving her family fortune to Woodrow. Then, only a matter of weeks earlier, young Frank Wilson had complained about his not being allowed to see the beautiful Elizabeth, Woodrow's daughter. Barker had been unable to help the rancher because Beth Woodrow was still legally a minor. Nothing about Jacob Woodrow seemed right.

Before Barker had time to speculate further his sore eyes spotted the citizens of Rio Concho as they started coming out in the morning sunlight. The few faces which glanced in his direction displayed nothing he had not seen before but today he simply could not face them.

The sheriff moved away from the window and closed the door, as if attempting to lock them out. His thoughts hovered on the still-attractive Donna Drumbar and her seductive words of comfort which he had never imagined might be aimed in his direction. Could she actually have been giving him a hint that she was available? It seemed impossible to the ageing sheriff. She was no spring chicken but still a damn sight younger than he was. Barker held onto the door-bolt and slid it across. Now he was certain they were locked out.

Now he was alone to brood.

His wrinkled hand pulled the cord of the shades down and the office was bathed in half-light once again. They could not see or bother him any more today. He was alone.

Barker opened the top right-hand drawer of his desk and pulled out a half-pint of bourbon. He would not step out into the street until he had consumed every last drop. This was one of those days that it was impossible to face with a clear head. Of late, there had been many of those days.

EIGHT

The impassive face of the butler Bates stared hard at the panting figure of Jacob Woodrow. He remembered when this sweating man had been as wealthy as his present master, but it only took one fleeting glance to know times had changed. Now Woodrow's clothes were frayed at the edges and the silk collar-trimmings no longer shone but lay lifeless against his neck.

'Is your master accepting visitors, Bates?' Woodrow asked the inscrutable man-servant.

'Mr O'Hara is awake but I shall have to enquire whether he is accepting callers, Mr Woodrow.' Bates stepped aside and pointed to a padded leather chair.

Woodrow took the hint and seated himself nervously whilst Bates marched off briskly into the depths of the house. It seemed an eternity to Woodrow as he stared at his thumbs, waiting for the butler to return.

Footsteps echoed around the vaulted hall as Bates returned and gestured for Woodrow to follow him. They seemed to weave their way through lavish drapes as they made their way through narrow corridors until they were out in the morning sunshine. Woodrow shielded his eyes with a plump hand as he trailed the slim-built servant up to the table and chairs where Jason O'Hara sat eating his breakfast.

'Thanks for seeing me, Jason,' Woodrow said as he accepted the chair Bates pulled out from the table.

'What brings you out at this hour, Woodrow?' O'Hara asked, pouring himself a coffee.

'You still hankering for my daughter?' The question cut through the air like a knife.

'What kind of question is that?' The businessman narrowly eyed the sweating, out-of-breath figure before him. He had detested the very sight of Jacob Woodrow since first he set eyes upon him. He knew instinctively whom he could and could not trust in Rio Concho and Woodrow fell into the latter category.

'May I have some juice, Jason?' Woodrow asked pointing to the large glass jug between them.

O'Hara nodded. 'Help yourself. What exactly are you getting at, Woodrow?'

There was a long pause as the older man poured himself a glass of juice and began sipping it.

'Woodrow!' O'Hara snapped, tossing his napkin into the middle of his breakfast plate.

Jacob Woodrow looked up with heavy-lidded eyes at the face opposite him. There was the slightest hint of a smile as he rested the glass on top of the table.

'You ain't made no secret of the fact you like my daughter, Jason. I just wondered how much you like her?'

O'Hara leaned back in his chair and studied Woodrow.

'I like her an awful lot, Jacob. Why?'

'No. I want to know, how much do you value her, Jason?' Woodrow eyed up the face of the man sitting opposite him.

'You sound as if you're selling something, Jacob. Are you trying to tell me Elizabeth is for sale?' O'Hara asked innocently.

'She is to the right man for the correct price, Jason.'

O'Hara looked into the unblinking eyes of his visitor and began to smile as he finally saw the true nature of someone he had always mistrusted.

'Well? Am I talking to the right man or

'not, Jason?' Woodrow asked coyly.

'You would sell your own daughter?' There was more than a little surprise in Jason O'Hara's voice.

'The question is, would you buy my daughter?' Jacob Woodrow took another gulp of the juice as he watched the face of the rich younger man. He had played many hands of poker over the previous decades and seen his once considerable wealth disappear into other men's wallets. Now he could not afford to lose this, his final game.

Jason O'Hara rose and moved around the table as if trying to distance himself from the creature who seemed to have even fewer scruples then he did.

'You've gone very quiet, Jason. Why?'

O'Hara sighed as he remembered how he had paid Zococa to go and kill Frank Wilson the previous evening. He knew Wilson was smitten with Beth Woodrow and feared it might be mutual. Yet that had not been the only reason he had paid hard cash to eliminate him. O'Hara had never done anything without there being a solid business motive behind it. There were two very different reasons for him wanting the young rancher out of the way.

Now it seemed as if one of the reasons why

he had wanted Wilson dead had evaporated into thin air.

'How does Beth feel about this?' O'Hara looked back at the man seated at his table. A man whom normally he would not even allow into his house.

'Her feelings have nothing to do with this,' said Woodrow with a heartless smirk.

O'Hara strode over to Woodrow and looked down at him.

'She ain't got no say in this?'

'None at all, Jason.' Woodrow meant what he said and it showed through his wrinkled mask of a face.

'I thought you didn't like me.'

'I don't like you, Jason. What I do like is your money.' The reply was honest if not palatable.

The younger man sat down again and looked hard at the plate with the crumpled napkin upon it. He seemed either unwilling or unable to look at Woodrow. However much he detested him, the idea of finally having the beautiful Beth for his wife was too good to pass up.

'You mentioned money, Jacob.'

'Correct.'

'How much money are you talking about, Jacob?' Jason O'Hara spoke with a concerned expression on his face; this was a question he had never thought would pass his lips.

'Ten thousand dollars.' Jacob Woodrow rose to his feet and began walking away. He had played his hand as best he could and now it was up to the younger man.

'Jacob.'

Woodrow paused and glanced over his shoulder. 'Well?'

'You got yourself a deal.'

'We have ourselves a big problem, *amigo*,' Zococa announced as he strode across the courtyard of the ranch towards the apple-orchard with the still confused Frank Wilson close at his heels.

'I can't see what problem you've got, Zococa. By my reckoning it's only me who's got himself trouble.'

The bandit reached up and pulled an apple from a heavily laden branch and began polishing it against his sleeve.

'I have been paid to kill you by *Señor* O'Hara and yet your sweetheart is afraid he will try and force her to marry him, I think.' Zococa looked at the young man with the doleful face. 'I might be only a villain but I am sure your Beth is a very innocent young girl. She is a prisoner and does not even know it. Now do you see my problem?'

For the first time since they had encountered one another Frank Wilson's face lit up.

'You've hit the nail on the head, Zococa. She's a damn prisoner in that house OK. Her father is a real strange dude and I got me a gut feeling he's planning something.'

'This was my theory also.' Zococa tossed the apple into the hands of the rancher.

'Ain't you gonna eat this?' Wilson asked, holding the apple out.

'Zococa does not eat the fruit, my young antelope. I am not a monkey.' The bandit began walking, his mind filled with a thousand riddles and not a single clue to solve any of their mysteries. A lesser man would have ridden away and not tried to get involved, but Zococa was not such a man.

The young rancher followed Zococa down across the fertile pastures until the bandit raised a hand and began sniffing the air.

'What is that stink, my fine young *amigo*?'

'Follow me and I'll show you,' Wilson said, walking through the tall grass with the reluctant bandit behind him.

'Are we going to the home of a skunk?' Zococa asked as he held his nose, trying to keep the stench from travelling further up his refined nostrils.

Frank Wilson stopped by some makeshift fencing and pointed down across the field of black goo which bubbled like a witches' cauldron. Gas vapour hung over the ground as if trapped by its own poisonous ambience.

'What is this?' Zococa queried.

'Some kinda tar pit, I figure.'

'We go. Pronto!' Zococa turned quickly and walked speedily away from the place which made his head spin.

'If I'd known about that chunk of swamp, I reckon I'd not have bought this little spread to start with,' said Wilson. He coughed as he finally caught up with the bandit.

'Has it always been like that, *amigo*?' Zococa bent over and gasped as they reached the fresher air nearer the house.

'Nope. It seems to be getting worse lately.'

Suddenly Zococa's face brightened as he remembered something buried deep within his memory.

'Now I recall, I have seen such a place before.'

'You have? Where?' Young Wilson seemed surprised that there could be another place as bad as his fenced-off field.

'A little ways north of here,' Zococa answered. 'I think they value this black mess.'

'What the hell for?'

Zococa shrugged. He had no answers which made any sense to his new-found friend nor to himself. The minds of the gringo businessmen far away in cities he had never even heard of were beyond his imagination. Yet he knew this terrible filth which blighted Frank Wilson's ranch was something which these men saw as valuable.

'I think crazy gringos use it for something.'

'Could it be worth enough to make a businessman like O'Hara pay to have me killed, Zococa?'

Frank Wilson looked at Zococa's smiling face.

Zococa rested a hand upon the shoulder of the rancher and grinned enigmatically.

'You are very smart, my fine chicken-lover.'

'Am I right though?'

'When I met this Jason O'Hara he did not seem the sort of man who would waste good money to have another killed just because he was in love, but if that black swamp is what I think it is, it makes a lot of sense.'

Zococa began heading for the small ranch house where Tahoka was waiting with a bowl of what was left of the fried chicken.

'What we going to do?' Wilson asked.

Zococa pulled out his silver cigar-case and offered one to the rancher, who refused. Zococa placed one of the dark smokes into his mouth, struck a match and puffed frantically.

'Do you have a plan?' Wilson looked at the bandit as he tossed his spent match away over his shoulder.

'The great Zococa does not require a plan, my simple one.'

Tahoka set the bowl of bones down and stood wiping the grease from his fingers onto his clothing as he stared at his partner knowingly.

'Quiet, my little giant,' Zococa said through the cigar smoke. 'I have decided to help our friend here. And his sweetheart.'

Tahoka looked at Wilson and made a handsign.

'What did he say?'

'He said I was loco.' Zococa laughed loudly. 'I think he knows me too well, *amigo*.'

NINE

There seemed to be a coldness drifting through the large house of Jason O'Hara as he walked silently into its heart. Drapes where none should have been hanging cast shadows and darkness which masked the lay-out of his abode. Yet this was how he wanted it and there was nobody to argue with his strange taste in décor. Nobody but one.

Opening a door which lay hidden behind one of the heavy drapes, the nervous businessman entered a room where no light penetrated. Jason O'Hara moved slowly to its centre and stopped when he felt the sharp corner of a wooden table against his upper thigh. Fumbling around, his hand found the back of a hard chair and he seated himself.

He sat in the blackness for what seemed an endless span of time. Only the single shaft of light slanting from the doorway gave his eyes something to focus upon. O'Hara tried, as he always tried, to relax. This was not a place to feel at ease though. Here, within the shifting variations of darkness, he never felt anything but raw terror. This was a room within his house, but it was not his room. He had long since given this sixteen-foot-square world to another and as he sat there waiting, as was his daily ritual, he felt the beads of sweat dripping from his brow. Then he heard the shuffling feet approaching from behind. Every hair on the back of his wide neck tingled as he sensed the figure getting closer and closer.

O'Hara knew there was no point in turning to look at the person who bore down upon him because he knew he would see nothing. This was a soul who lived in the darkness for reasons too horrific to think about even for more than a fleeting moment.

Jason O'Hara did not need to be told why this being chose to hide within this room, for the reason was known to him alone and if his companion chose to exist this way, it was a choice he understood, even if he found it more than a little unnerving.

'We had a visitor, Jason?' the voice said.

'Jacob Woodrow was just here,' O'Hara said in his usual well-spoken manner, giving no clue as to how terrifying he always found these daily encounters.

'Good. So you have managed finally to tempt the fly into our web, Jason. I knew the aroma of money was too great for him to ignore.' The voice was deep and yet somehow fragile.

'He's told me he wants me to buy his daughter.' O'Hara cleared his throat as he spoke.

'This I knew would happen. It has come sooner than I had expected, though. Still, now we can turn the screw on the bastard.' The figure swept like a breeze around the chair where O'Hara sat.

'He wants ten thousand dollars,' O'Hara said as he tried to avert his eyes from the direction of the voice.

'An agreeable sum, Jason,' the deep tones mused as the figure paused behind the hard chair once again.

'I'm getting a little concerned. Are you certain we have to go through with this?' The question seemed to fall into the dust at O'Hara's feet.

'Are you doubting my plan, Jason?' O'Hara fancied he heard a slight modulation in the voice.

'No. You have always known best but I'm getting worried.'

'Why? Have I not always steered you along the right path? Do you recall what you were before you met me?' The voice was closer now and every word seemed to ruffle O'Hara's hair.

He bowed humbly. 'I do not need reminding how you made me what I am today.'

'Good. For what I have given, I can take back, Jason.' There was more than a hint of a threat as these words brushed over the skin of the listener.

O'Hara rubbed his hand over his face as he sensed his companion standing closer behind him than he cared for.

'Did I have to hire the bandit Zococa to kill the rancher?'

'Yes. This was part of my overall strategy. We require the crude oil which is on his property. Killing Frank Wilson means we can purchase the deeds from the bank out of the goodness of our hearts. If we act quickly, they will not need to have the land surveyed. If we were to try and buy the property from Wilson legally, someone might discover the black gold pumping up out of the ground and put two and two together.'

O'Hara nodded.

'What has old man Woodrow got to do

with all this?'

'That, Jason, like everything else, you will discover in due course. Now you will pay a visit with Jacob and his beautiful daughter. You will not, however, take the money he wants. Not yet.' The voice began to fade as the figure moved into a corner.

The audience was over, and O'Hara knew it was time for him to leave. He rose to his feet and moved towards the thin shaft of light at the door. Without looking back, he left the room, closing the door firmly behind him. His heart was still pounding as he made his way into the rear gardens.

It was almost noon as the two riders pulled at their reins and slowed their horses to a trot. Zococa and his faithful friend Tahoka were well aware that it was dangerous for them to enter any town during the hours of daylight, but they were confident in the security their admirers offered them as they wove their way along the sweet-smelling avenues of Rio Concho.

The bandit chewed on a cigar which had ceased burning long ago as his eyes darted about them. Zococa saw everything and missed nothing. Sitting proudly astride his pinto stallion as he headed with Tahoka towards their favourite cantina, where they knew they could take a couple of hours' rest, Zococa felt uneasy. He had never been in such a complicated web of deceit before, and he seemed unable to turn his broad back on the innocent young souls he had met. Beth Woodrow was the most exquisite female he had ever come across and, although he wanted her, he knew her heart belonged to Frank Wilson. For his part, young Frank Wilson was a simple man but hard working and honest. Perhaps it was the eternal romantic in his nature but Zococa had decided that it was his duty to bring these two innocents together.

Somehow Jason O'Hara held the key to it all but as yet the bandit had not worked out how or why. The pair of love-sick youngsters were vulnerable to the vultures which circled above them. Their purity was their downfall. It was said, it took a thief to catch a thief, and Zococa had no equal when it came to outwitting even the most ruthless of men.

Zococa knew Wilson's and Beth's only chance of survival lay in his unworthy hands. It was a new experience for the bandit but he liked the way it made him feel. For the first time in his life he found himself championing less able souls.

Tahoka reined in first as they drew closer to the rickety hitching rail outside the cantina but he did not dismount until Zococa nodded.

They tied their mounts securely whilst their eyes darted around the quiet alley, seeking any sign of trouble. There was none. This part of Rio Concho appeared to be asleep.

'Do not worry, my little elephant. It is siesta time and the sun is high. Only the crazy Americanos walk out in the afternoon sun.' Zococa grinned.

The Apache pointed to the bandit and himself.

'I agree. We are also loco but soon we shall be able to take the rest.' Zococa smiled as he stepped onto the boardwalk and yawned discreetly. As he patted his mouth his keen eyesight spotted the familiar small boy standing on a nearby corner watching them.

'Look, Tahoka. It is the brave one from last night who brought us the note from *Señor* O'Hara.' Zococa lifted his hand and curled his finger at the child. 'Come here, my little *vaquero*. The great Zococa would speak with you.'

The boy rushed up to the bandit and grinned.

'It is good to see the great Zococa has not been killed since we last met,' the boy said, holding out his hand and displaying the bullet.

'What did I tell you yesterday, my brave one?' Zococa asked.

'You said you would give me two silver dollars for this bullet, *señor.*' The reply came swiftly from the confident child.

Zococa rubbed his neck as he thought.

'I will not give you two silver dollars for this bullet but I will give you a five-dollar bill if you will take our horses to the small stable behind the cantina and guard them for a couple of hours.'

'Should I also remove their saddles and rub them down, great Zococa?' The boy looked up at the two men without a single quiver of fear showing in his little face.

'For this, Zococa will give you two five-dollar bills, my fearless one.' The bandit reached into his jacket and withdrew two five-dollar bills. He handed them to the boy and took back his bullet.

'I shall also warn you if I sense even the slightest danger, O great bandit.' The boy's eyes flashed as he spoke.

Zococa laughed as he entered the cantina with his friend at his side.

'That child will go far, my little hippopotamus.'

Tahoka grunted.

'He has the spirit like myself. It is the courage so few have but which I seem to be blessed with in great abundance. Do you not agree?' Zococa looked at the face of his friend. As usual, only the eyes moved as they rolled upwards seeking assistance from a greater source.

'Zococa!' The voice of the attractive Conchita rang out across the cantina as the two tired men pushed through the beaded hanging drape.

'Conchita!' Zococa smiled, holding out his arms as the woman came rushing towards him.

'You have returned so soon, my handsome one.' Her soft voice seemed to sigh as she wrapped herself around him like a vine.

'I could not stay away; you dragged my soul across the prairie with your perfume.' Zococa tossed his sombrero across the room as he scooped her up in his arms and stared deeply into her large brown eyes.

'My perfume?'

'It is the smell of desire, Conchita. You

ooze it from every beautiful pore of your soft skin.' Zococa buried his lips in her neck and kissed her feverishly. He could feel her heart beating beneath his skilled lips.

'Do we make love now?' Conchita breathed as she heaved her bosom up into his smiling face.

'I did come here to rest for a couple of hours but...' Zococa suddenly felt refreshed as he rained kisses over her firm breasts which tumbled out of her low cut blouse.

'We have rooms upstairs. Rooms with beds,' Conchita gasped as she climbed up his body and hung about his neck.

'I think we require only one room and one bed, my shy little Conchita.' The bandit could feel the explosive heat of her body as she became overwhelmed by his famous lovemaking skills.

'Take me to heaven, Zococa!' Conchita screamed as the bandit carried her across the cantina and ascended the stairs with her clinging willingly to him.

Tahoka sat down by a table and watched as the pair disappeared into the first open doorway at the top of the stairs. He shook his head slowly as the mother walked up to him smiling.

'My little Conchita has met her match, I

think,' she said, smiling, to the tired Apache.

Tahoka looked at her with his usual blank expression.

'Is Tahoka hungry?' she asked.

He nodded.

TEN

'Did you get any sleep, my little giant?' Zococa asked the tall Indian as they left the cantina and crossed the alley. Tahoka nodded. 'You are most fortunate.'

Tahoka used his nimble fingers to ask the bandit if he had managed to get any rest.

Zococa shrugged as he donned his sombrero. 'There was no time; the lovely Conchita kept me so busy. She is very strong and every time I tried to get forty winks, she started making love to me once more. I am but a slave to these amorous ladies, *amigo*.'

Tahoka shook his head at his smiling friend. There seemed to be a Conchita in every town they visited together. Sometimes there were far more than just one. It was a mystery now and then to the Apache how the bandit managed to retain enough strength to get from one town to the next.

'Do not disapprove *pequeño*. Am I to break their hearts by refusing to make love to them? I am not strong willed like you.'

Zococa pinched the cheek of his partner's face but there was no hint that the brave Apache felt anything.

Zococa and Tahoka walked through the winding alleys slowly. Both men were weary and on the point of exhaustion as they approached the gates of the Woodrow mansion. Tahoka had slept, it was true, but only briefly on a hard chair after he had eaten.

It was now nearly five in the afternoon and the bright sun had dipped low enough in the blue sky to cast long shadows all across Rio Concho. The pair had used every shadow on their journey to this place.

The bandit had paused beside some bushes for a moment as if to collect his thoughts when Tahoka suddenly pulled him back into the depths of the shadows.

The Apache looked at his partner before dropping to his knees and resting the palm of his left hand on the dry soil. His eyes stared up at Zococa.

'Is someone coming?' the bandit asked as Tahoka got back to his feet and put his fingers to his mouth. His hands spoke to the eyes of the tired Mexican far more vividly than any spoken words could ever have done. Zococa nodded as he read the signals of his mute friend.

Just then a large coach drawn by a magnificent pair of matched chestnut geldings passed in front of them. The Apache held firmly onto Zococa's shoulders as he assessed the situation.

'Do not be afraid *amigo*. I, the great Zococa, am here to protect you.' The bandit sighed as he peered out from the shadows to see the coach pulling up outside the locked gates of Jacob Woodrow's house.

Tahoka released his grip as he too ventured to take a look at the stationary coach.

'That is a very splendid vehicle, is it not?' Zococa noted as he watched the driver climbing down from his high seat and opening the black lacquered door.

To both men's utter surprise, the unmistakable figure of Jason O'Hara stepped down from the carriage onto the boardwalk. He was dressed in his finest clothes and wearing a dark silk top-hat. In his gloved hands he carried a walking-cane with a hand-crafted silver top and tip. No man dressed this way to attend a business meeting, Zococa thought. O'Hara looked as if he had come courting.

'Now I am beginning to understand a few things, Tahoka,' the bandit said as he watched Jacob Woodrow unlocking the gates and greeting the businessman. It was obvious by the expression upon O'Hara's face that he did not like Woodrow but had to observe the usual formalities.

O'Hara followed the older man in through the gates.

'We are too far away to hear what they are saying, little one,' Zococa whispered.

Tahoka nodded in agreement as they carefully edged their way along the street, trying to remain in the safety of the dark shadows. Pressing their backs into the high wall both men moved beneath the canopy of overhanging leafy branches, watching as the coach-driver climbed back to his high seat. As the carriage moved away and proceeded into the distance, Zococa gave a huge sigh of relief and followed the silent Apache towards the gates.

'The way *Señor* O'Hara was so prettily dressed, I think he has the lovemaking on his mind, Tahoka. This I cannot allow to happen.' Zococa licked his dry lips and tasted the remnants of the lip paint of the lovely Conchita once again. For a moment his mind drifted back to the cantina.

The stony-faced Apache gave an annoyed grunt as he peered at the locked gates –

gates which Jacob Woodrow had secured after admitting his guest.

'Is it locked, my little rhinoceros?' Zococa asked his tall companion. 'This is most annoying for my plans. I had intended sneaking up the pathway to the house.'

Tahoka made a pained, frustrated expression as he lifted his pistol from its holster and aimed at the sturdy chains wrapped around the iron bars.

Zococa reached out and forced Tahoka's pistol down from its chosen target.

'No, no, little one. We cannot use our guns to shoot the padlock off the gates. This I think would be noticed.' The bandit carefully steered his partner's weapon back into its leather holster.

'I wish we had brought the horses. This is a very high wall to climb without the help of a saddle to stand upon.' Zococa frowned as he stared up at the overhanging branches of the tree.

Without a second's hesitation, Tahoka bent down and gripped his partner's legs. Zococa gritted his teeth as he felt the strength of the Apache. As Tahoka swiftly rose back to an upright position, the bandit was thrown up into the mighty tree's branches.

Leaves floated gently down over the imperturbable warrior. Gazing upward, Tahoka saw Zococa smile broadly before he disappeared into the heart of the stalwart tree.

ELEVEN

Sheriff Bob Barker moved through the Scotsman Saloon like a mere phantom of his former self. He felt old now. The liquor had done nothing to help either his own feelings of frustration or his lack of sleep. As he approached the long mahogany bar with its brass foot- and elbow-rails he staggered and slumped into a pyramid of stacked whiskey-glasses.

Each and every eye fell upon the back of the sheriff as he regained his balance and tried to ignore the muffled laughter that rippled all around him in the crowded saloon.

She moved as she had always done, effortlessly and with a confidence not always found in women of her reputation. Donna Drumbar might have only been a mere four feet eleven inches in height but she commanded total respect in this, her private world. No living man or woman dared to cross swords with her because she would never allow it. There were few females so utterly in tune with their own souls that they lived to an inner music no other could hear. Hers had always been a hard life and yet she had managed to overcome everything the world had thrown at her. No obstacle had ever slowed her progress through a life filled with colour and adventure, yet now she felt it had reached its conclusion. No longer did she wish to be what she had spent a lifetime becoming. Now things had to change because she was beginning to change.

There comes a time in all women's lives when they have to face one simple truth. They are no longer young.

Donna Drumbar had reached this time and now she looked forward to a day when only old age remained to be conquered and death, its sad alternative, delayed. What she saw in the weathered sheriff who clung to the brass elbow-bar, trying not to fall into the array of spittoons, only she knew. Maybe it was his honesty. It might have been the fact he had never shirked trouble and, like herself, was afraid of no living person. Whatever the reason for her finding herself drawn to the man who looked all the worse for wear after consuming a half-bottle of whiskey, she could not help herself from moving to him.

'You OK, Bob?' Her words seemed to make his strength return to his legs and he found himself standing unaided beside her.

'Drunk, Miss Drumbar. I'm just drunk.' He sighed heavily as he felt her pressing against him.

'Why do you do this to yourself, Bob?' she asked.

'Maybe it's all getting a mite tough, ma'am.' He shrugged as he found himself looking down into her beautiful face.

'Then quit.' Her words were blunt and yet posed a question he had never even considered before.

'Quit?' Barker pushed his hat back from his face and looked down into her heavily painted features. As he stared at her through his blurred eyes he began to see her as few had ever done. No amount of make-up could disguise the beauty which had lain hidden for so very many years.

'Yes. Quit or retire. Just stop chasing something you can never catch, Bob. Sometimes folks have to face some hard facts.' She took his arm and led him towards her own private table set in a corner, where she had an unhindered view of her saloon's interior.

Barker sat down and buried his face in his hands. 'I'm old, ma'am. Too damn old.'

'The name's Donna, and you ain't alone.' Her face smiled the smile of a woman who knew more than she would ever admit.

'You ain't old, Donna.' The sheriff held her hand and patted it tenderly.

'Old enough to know I can't ever re-capture my lost youth.'

He did not understand. 'I reckon you're right. I ought to quit.'

'We could start a new life together here in Rio Concho. Two old wrecks together.' She smiled as she saw the figure of Ben Francis, the banker, moving towards them.

'Barker,' the voice of the banker boomed.

The sheriff looked up and stared at the red-faced man.

'What do you want, Ben?'

'Haven't you heard?'

'Heard what?'

'Go away, Ben.' Donna Drumbar inter-rupted.

'Zococa has been spotted in town, you drunken fool.' Francis shouted angrily.

'He's in my town?' Bob Barker rose to his feet angrily.

'Let it be, Bob,' Donna Drumbar pleaded with the man who could hear nothing but the laughter of the bandit which had mocked him so many times.

'He might be here to rob my bank, Sheriff. What are you going to do?' Ben Francis leaned into the lawman as he spoke.

'Zococa is in my town? The young rooster ain't got no damn respect.' Barker pulled away from Donna and staggered past the banker.

'But, Bob. Why?' Donna Drumbar tried to stop Barker but it was impossible.

'Because I'm the sheriff, Donna,' he said as he made his way out into the street.

Donna Drumbar stood and pushed a finger into the chest of the banker and warned, 'You better pray he don't get himself killed, Ben. Because if he does, I'm coming gunning for you.'

Walking across the wide branches of the gigantic tree, and hidden by the dense foliage, Zococa reached the spot where, the previous night, he had first encountered the lovely Beth Woodrow. Holding onto the higher branches, the bandit carefully pushed aside the leaves to see exactly where he was. There was no sign of O'Hara or Woodrow and the huge garden beneath him appeared deserted. Then, directly level with his dangerously high perch, Zococa noticed an open bedroom window.

Zococa edged his feet cautiously along a six-inch-wide branch as he gripped at thin hanging leafy vines. The branch beneath his feet began to sag under the strain of his weight, forcing Zococa to take one step backwards. The window was wide open, allowing the room to air, and was only about five feet away from where he was balancing.

This was Beth's room, Zococa thought. Her unique perfume drifted into his nostrils as he balanced, trying to get a better view. He removed his sombrero, hung it on a branch and ran his fingers through his black hair as he prepared himself.

Zococa leaned out as far as he dared and stared inside the room. It was empty, but Beth's fragrance remained even though she was not there. There were many frills and pink things adorning it. Beth had branded this room with her very soul and he could feel himself being drawn to it just as he had been attracted to the ravishing female herself.

Zococa took a deep breath and began rocking back and forth, trying to get the leverage which he would need when he leapt out from the tree towards the open window.

After only the fourth backward sway on his high heels, Zococa sprang like a puma out of the dense green foliage and flew at the building.

Somehow he managed to land both his feet on the wide window-sill and grappled the open window frames with both hands. After a few seconds he lowered himself silently into the bedroom and looked around, studying everything in view. Inhaling deeply, he once more seemed to be filled with the subtle aroma of the girl with the golden hair. It was like a drug to his weary senses. A drug which gave him renewed vigour.

As he stood on the thick carpet his keen hearing caught voices coming from downstairs through the slightly ajar door.

Zococa walked slowly to the door and listened to the raised voices. Going out onto the wide landing he stared over a wooden balustrade into a huge room, unlike any he had ever seen before. It was at least thirty feet square with long windows facing south. Its walls were panelled in wood and there were three long couches set around a slim table. Only Beth Woodrow was seated. Jason O'Hara was standing toe to toe with an older man who, Zococa assumed, was the infamous Jacob Woodrow. They were shouting at one another angrily while the passive golden haired beauty sat watching.

It took a few moments before Zococa was able to understand what they were saying to one another. The argument was so heated it seemed to the bandit that a fight could occur at any moment.

It concerned money. Zococa clenched his fists as he began to understand what the two men had apparently agreed between themselves at an earlier meeting.

It was ugly. Obscene.

They were discussing Beth as if she were a mere object to be bought and sold. The Mexican could hardly believe his ears at how low some men could stoop in their total disregard for those less strong than themselves.

Zococa felt the fire within his soul beginning to burn again; his own fury grew with every word that left either man's foul mouth and he began toying with his silver-plated pistol. His thumb flicked off the safety loop and he rested his palm on the grip as he tried to control his anger.

Just as he was about to pull the weapon from its holster and storm down into the room, Beth screamed hysterically and rose to her feet. The two men paused and looked in her direction as she burst into tears and ran towards the staircase.

Zococa moved backwards into the bedroom as she came running up the flight of stairs. He hid behind the door as Beth rushed in and slammed the door behind her. He stood watching her sobbing helplessly. Her eyes were flooded with tears as she staggered across the room and fell upon the bed.

Zococa slid the bolt on the door and waited.

Beth turned her red face in his direction and tried to speak through the gasps of emotion.

The bandit put a finger to his lips and walked towards her, trying to smile so she would know everything was OK. For the first time since Silver Springs, Zococa could not smile.

His heart was pounding as he reached her side. He seemed to feel her pain as if it were his own. Kneeling down, he looked into her eyes as he rested his elbows upon the soft bed.

'My little golden one must not cry so. The great Zococa is here for you.'

'Zococa!' She flung her arms around his

neck and tried to gain strength from his simply being there. He patted her back gently as he wondered why anyone could be so cruel to such a delicate creature.

Running his hand over her hair he knew this was no game he could play whilst laughing. This had a deadly seriousness about it which troubled the normally care-free man.

'What did they say?'

'My father demanded money from Jason O'Hara.' She shook in his arms as she talked. 'I don't understand. He said they had agreed the sum of ten thousand dollars. What does it mean?'

'Your father has sold you to *Señor* O'Hara, my little one.'

'Sold me?'

Zococa tried to be as kind as he could but the words were uglier than any which, until now, had soured his mouth.

'You are to be the bride. Ten thousand dollars is the price.'

Her face seemed utterly drained as she tried to cope with the horror of her plight. She knew her father had been acting even more strangely than usual of late, but could he actually be willing to trade her for a price?

'I must go now, Beth. There is much to do.' Zococa reluctantly pulled away from her and stood next to the open window casting his attention down into the luxuriant garden.

'Did you get to see Frank? Is he well?' Though Beth Woodrow's face was stained with tears it was yet more beautiful than any other he had set eyes upon.

'I saw him and he is well.' Zococa nodded as he found himself envying another man for the first time in his life. Frank Wilson might not have much money, Zococa thought, but he had the heart of this young woman.

'What is going on, Zococa? I'm so confused.' Beth's eyes darted around the room as if even here there was no safety for her.

'The answers to this lie in another place, my bright flower.' The bandit leaned out of the window and watched as the two arguing men moved to the gates. His keen eyes looked on as Jacob Woodrow unlocked the padlock and allowed O'Hara to leave the property just as the sumptuous carriage pulled up at the gates.

'My father says I must marry Jason O'Hara.' Her voice shook as she spoke.

'This, I promise, will never happen.'

Zococa held her shoulders and looked into her face. Somehow he managed to pull himself away from her before climbing onto the window-sill.

'Zococa?'

'I shall return,' Zococa said as he sprang away from the house and vanished among the branches of the great tree.

TWELVE

The fierce sun had set and at long last Rio
Concho became bearable once more.
Zococa struck a match and lit his cigar
before passing the flame to Tahoka's. Both
men puffed for a few moments as they
approached Jason O'Hara's house. There
were few lights along this quiet street and
that suited both men.

'I am having the confusion, my little elephant,' Zococa said as he stared at the house.

Tahoka chewed on the cigar as smoke
poured from his wide nostrils. He wanted to
leave this place and take the money they had
tricked from O'Hara.

'For the first time, I have to admit I am
not sure what is going on, Tahoka,' the
bandit admitted as he rested his back
against a tree trunk and savoured the
flavour of his cigar. 'I do not know whom to
confront, *amigo*. Who is the true baddie? I
think they are all as bad as one another.'

Tahoka gestured with his hands once
again.

'Be quiet, my noisy one. You are giving me another of my headaches with all your chattering.' Zococa released the knot on his hat string and allowed his sombrero to fall back.

The two men moved closer to the house.

'I think we should go inside and have the talk with the very nasty *Señor* O'Hara. What do you think, little one?' Zococa looked at his partner who was shaking his head.

Tahoka kept level with the bandit as they approached the house.

Suddenly Zococa stopped, held out a hand and touched the chest of the tall Apache.

'You go and get the horses from the cantina, Tahoka. I shall enter alone.'

The warrior frowned and shook his hands frantically at the Mexican.

Zococa laughed. 'I will be OK. You get yourself a meal and wait for me. I think we might have to go back to the rancho of Frank Wilson a little later.'

Reluctantly, the Apache left his friend's side and disappeared into the darkness of the quiet street. Zococa flicked the ash off his cigar as he wondered what lay ahead of him inside this house. He tossed the cigar away and drew his pistol before moving to the side of the building.

Jason O'Hara was standing beside the large table waiting for Bates to bring him his evening meal when he heard the door behind him opening.

'Put the food down and leave, Bates,' O'Hara said masterfully.

There was no reply. Only footsteps which moved confidently up behind him.

O'Hara turned, expecting to see his butler, only to be greeted by the smiling Zococa holding his gun.

'Zococa!' the businessman gasped.

'Well observed, *señor*.'

'I ... I did not expect to see you. You startled me.' Jason O'Hara moved to a chair and sat down. He was stunned to find that the bandit could enter his home so easily. 'How did you get in? The doors are usually locked after dark.'

'They were locked OK.' Zococa nodded in agreement. 'But I have never met the door which I cannot open, *Señor* O'Hara.'

'Did you complete the little job for me?' The businessman tried to calm his shattered nerves by pouring himself a glass of wine from an open bottle set upon the table next to his chair.

'This is most embarrassing.' Zococa raised

both his eyebrows as he replaced his gun in its holster and sat on the corner of the long dining-table.

'I do not understand,' O'Hara said, as he held the glass to his dry lips.

'You see, things sometimes happen which change my plans.'

'Have you killed Wilson?' The voice of the seated man was becoming louder and less rational.

'Not exactly, my friend.' Zococa shrugged.

'He still lives?' O'Hara took a mouthful of his wine and swallowed hard. It did not help.

'*Sì*. He still lives.'

'But why? I paid you five hundred dollars to kill him.' O'Hara expostulated as if hiring assassins was an everyday occurrence and perfectly respectable.

'Do you think I am not grateful for the funds which you so generously gave to me and my faithful friend Tahoka, but things have changed, *amigo*.' Zococa placed the index finger of his right hand on his lips as he watched the discomfited O'Hara downing the remainder of his wine.

'How have they changed?' O'Hara yelled.

'You did not tell me about the oil which is on Frank Wilson's land, *amigo*.' Zococa smiled as he watched O'Hara's expression change with every throbbing heartbeat.

'Oil? I know nothing about any oil, Zococa.' O'Hara felt the blood rise to his cheeks as he tried to face down the Mexican.

'You are a very good liar, *señor*. But I am the son of Mexico's greatest teller of tall stories and cannot be fooled.' Zococa rested the palm of his left hand upon the grip of his pistol as he watched O'Hara squirming.

O'Hara lowered his head. 'What difference does the oil make to you anyway?'

'It makes a great deal of difference; now Frank Wilson is rich and as such can afford to hire the great Zococa to kill you instead.' The face of the bandit beamed as he spoke. He had found the game once more and was milking it for every juicy drop of its splendid flavour.

'Wilson has no money, Zococa. How could he hire a bandit such as yourself?' O'Hara swallowed hard as he watched the calm Mexican before him enjoying every second of their vocal confrontation.

'I give him credit, *señor*.'

There was a hushed silence in the large room as the two men looked at each other. O'Hara knew he was holding onto a stick of

117

dynamite with its fuse lit. Zococa was no simple hired gun like the usual rabble O'Hara used to do his dirty work. The bandit was smarter and far more complicated than he had ever imagined and it scared him.

'Are you serious about killing me?' the businessman managed to ask as he helped himself to the last of his wine.

'We have many questions to ask each other, *amigo*.' Zococa grinned as he spoke. It was an even wider, broader grin than he normally displayed.

'Questions?'

'*Sî.* Why were you at the house of the lovely Beth Woodrow earlier?' Zococa ran his finger and thumb over his neatly trimmed moustache.

Jason O'Hara suddenly became nervous. How much more of his business did this man know?'

'I just had to complete a deal with her father. Why?'

'You are most sad.' Zococa frowned as he watched O'Hara reaching for the pull-cord next to his chair and tugging it.

'I wonder what's keeping my dinner?' O'Hara said to himself as he tried desperately to work out how much Zococa knew.

'Forget your stomach, *señor*. You must explain to Zococa why you are trying to buy yourself a wife.'

O'Hara gritted his teeth as he glared at Zococa.

Both men looked up as Bates the butler entered the room carrying a large silver tray. For a moment he seemed to hesitate as he saw the bandit but then continued towards the table.

'I see your food has arrived, *amigo*.' Zococa smiled as Bates moved behind him with the heavy tray.

Jason O'Hara rose to his feet and returned the smile.

'Thank you, Bates.'

Zococa began to turn his head when he felt the cold steel gun-barrel against his neck as the well-trained servant cocked its hammer.

'Make one move and I'll blow your head off your shoulders, sir,' Bates said stiffly.

'I think Bates is a very good butler, my friend.' Zococa cleared his throat as he felt his silver-plated pistol being removed from his holster.

The crashing blow which caught the bandit across the back of his head and neck sent him stumbling to the centre of the room before he fell face down at Jason O'Hara's feet.

'There is none better, Zococa,' O'Hara laughed.

THIRTEEN

The face of the Apache brave seldom showed any sign of emotion but as he reached and entered the cantina, Tahoka's jaw dropped in surprise. The beaded drapes swung back and forth noisily as he became aware that he was standing a few feet away from the sheriff whom he knew was called Bob Barker, who had been questioning Conchita and her mother. The cantina was occupied by fewer than a dozen souls but everyone of them was looking directly at the startled Tahoka.

Sheriff Barker turned away from Conchita and her mother and approached Tahoka.

'Don't see many Indians in Rio Concho,' the sheriff noted as he walked around the huge man with some curiosity.

Conchita forced a concerned smile across her lips and walked to the side of Tahoka. She grabbed his hand.

'Come on. You are late,' she said, dragging him towards the cooking area of the cantina.

Bob Barker rested a hand upon the

shoulder of the Apache and turned him around to face him. There was no obvious emotion in the dark tanned face as it focused on the lawman.

'Who are you, boy?' Barker asked as he tried to remember where he had seen the strangely silent man before.

Tahoka's eyes flashed from the lawman to the attractive young woman who held tightly onto his sweating hand, before he returned his attention to its original target.

'Cat got ya tongue?' Barker pressed.

'He does not speak very good English, Sheriff.' Conchita interrupted as she deliberately ran her free hand over her thin white blouse, trying to divert the older man's thoughts.

For the briefest of moments, Conchita saw the wrinkled eyes of the sheriff glancing at her firm erect nipples as they pushed at the flimsy fabric.

'What's an Indian doing in your cantina, Mamá Gomez?' Barker glanced at Conchita's mother.

The stout woman stepped closer to the trio.

'Conchita is so big-hearted, *señor*. She told me she had hired a new dish-washer but did not tell me he was an Indian,' she explained.

122

'You a dish-washer, son? You don't look like no dish-washer to me with that fancy pistol hanging on your hip,' the sheriff said to Tahoka.

'I gave him my late Pedro's gun to wear in case there is trouble in the cantina, Sheriff,' Mamá Gomez explained hurriedly.

'How come you don't talk, sonny?' Barker pressed the motionless Apache.

Tahoka felt Conchita's small hand squeeze his own as he tried to think of what to do next.

'He only speaks Mexican, Sheriff,' Conchita said, trying to lead Tahoka away from the shrewd lawman. 'This is why he washes dishes. I told him he has to learn English if he wants to better himself.'

'Reckon you're right, Conchita.' Barker nodded and released his grip upon the large Apache. He watched as he was taken into the rear of the cantina.

'I never seen such a big Indian,' he announced to the smiling woman beside him.

'My Conchita says he is a very good dish-washer, Sheriff. He breaks nothing,' Mamá Gomez said as she felt her heart beginning to beat normally once more.

Barker pushed the curtain beads apart and

paused for a moment in the doorway. His face was grim and reflected the bitterness he felt for the elusive bandit who had made his life a misery over the past few years.

'What troubles you?' Conchita's mother asked.

Barker looked hard into the plump face which, he remembered, was once even prettier than her daughter's. He touched her cheek and then looked out into the dark alley. Barker knew that Zococa was out there somewhere, probably planning his next job which would be yet another humiliation to weigh heavily upon his shoulders.

'Zococa is out there, Mamá Gomez. I gotta catch him. This time I just gotta catch him.' There was a desperation in the voice of the sheriff. He felt as if he had one last opportunity to salvage his reputation.

'You will do your best, Sheriff,' Mamá Gomez said softly as the lawman marched out into the shadows defiantly. Turning, she looked across the cantina at the faces of her daughter and the mute Tahoka.

'Is he gone, *Mamá?*' Conchita asked quietly.

'For now, Conchita. For now,' came the sombre reply.

It had taken far longer than Frank Wilson had thought for him to reach the outskirts of Rio Concho. His lumbering plough-horse was sturdy but not bred for speed or comfort. It had taken the young rancher most of the long afternoon, riding bareback astride his huge horse, but no hardship could deter him. The words of Zococa had haunted him. Wilson knew the bandit had a habit of exaggerating but felt he would not deliberately lie. Dragging at the makeshift reins, Wilson stopped the huge mount outside the chained gates of the Woodrow mansion and stared up at the house he had grown to hate.

The young man studied the locked gates with a mixture of rage and trepidation filling his knotted stomach. Were they chained to keep him out or Beth trapped inside?

He intended to confront the strange Jacob Woodrow before this night was through. For too long he had allowed the man to do as he wished without ever standing up to the grim figure. He knew the law was on the side of Beth's father but sometimes the law was blind to truth.

If Zococa was correct, there was little time left; no time to be wasted on the diplomacies of a young man vainly asking a parent for his daughter's hand in marriage.

Sitting on the broad-backed horse, Wilson felt scared of what lay within the great house. Unlike himself, Woodrow had guns and a reputation for being able and willing to use them. All Wilson had was his own sense of justice. Jacob Woodrow was no man to confront greenly.

The youthful rancher had once been allowed inside the house when Woodrow had not yet noticed his daughter's blossoming womanhood; had not considered her value. It seemed a lifetime had passed since those days when he and Beth had been free to love.

Could he face such a man, Wilson wondered? Was there even the slightest chance of freeing his sweetheart from this prison Woodrow had created?

Every passing second drove doubts into Wilson's mind which felt like six inch nails being hammered into his skull. He was afraid and had good reason to be. Jacob Woodrow was no ordinary man but a soul tormented by his own evil past.

It took more than youth to face such an adversary. It took a person who, unlike Woodrow himself, had not been tainted by selfishness.

Yet Frank Wilson was no hero like Zococa. He had none of the smiling bandit's skills or bravado to back him up. All he had was the doubts any sane man would hold within his breast.

Was it possible to help Beth?

Then he saw the glass globe-lamp being lit in her bedroom window. He felt his fears evaporate as he stared up at her silhouette. She moved to the window but did not see him below in the dark street.

For an instant young Frank Wilson felt as if he ought to cry out to her but knew any such outburst might also find other less attractive ears.

Like countless men before him, Frank Wilson, found himself defying his own fears and finding an inner strength where none had previously existed.

Urging the massive horse up beside the high gates, Wilson carefully used the creature's height to boost himself up and over the iron railings. He dropped to the ground within the dark property and moved like a moth towards the light from the high window.

FOURTEEN

If ever a man showed caution it was Jason O'Hara as he knocked upon the door hidden behind the heavy drapes. He turned the handle, stepped into the darkened room and stood trying to calm his nerves.

'What is it, Jason?' the voice asked quietly from the furthest corner.

'Zococa. He showed up and started causing trouble.' O'Hara remained close to the door as he saw the shimmering image moving about in the gloom.

'What sort of trouble?' the voice enquired.

'He knew about the oil on the Wilson ranch.' Jason O'Hara felt the sweat running down his face and into his collar.

'Has he killed Wilson?' The figure seemed to be getting closer with every word.

'No. He said he was going to kill me instead. The guy is tricky. I can't figure him out.'

'What have you done about our tricky friend?' The question brushed O'Hara's cheek as the figure glided past.

'Bates cracked him over the skull. He's out for the count.' O'Hara heard himself chuckle as he recalled the sight of Zococa having his skull cracked open.

'Good.' There seemed a genuine approval in the voice. 'Wilson's land would have been a profitable addition to our holdings but it does not matter any more.'

'What should we do with Zococa? Kill him?'

'Not yet, Jason.' The figure moved behind O'Hara.

'I don't like this.' The businessman felt his skin beginning to crawl as he felt the apparently shapeless form leaning against him.

'Your likes and dislikes are beside the point. You will do exactly as I order,' the voice said calmly.

'This whole thing is out of control.' O'Hara swallowed deeply.

'I am still in control, Jason.' The words were confident and strong as they touched the taller man's ear.

'But I'm worried.' Jason O'Hara felt terror racing through him as he looked down and back at the door.

'I am not.' The figure moved to the opposite side of the room and leaned against the wall.

'Jacob Woodrow blew his top when I showed up without the money earlier. He was like a madman,' O'Hara admitted as he watched the confused shape.

'Then you did your job well. I wanted Woodrow angry and confused so he would be off guard, Jason.' The words were tinged with a hint of humour as they wafted across the room.

'I don't like none of this. You forget I'm the fall guy. You make all the decisions and I'm the man who gets fingers pointed at him.' O'Hara tried to step forward but his feet felt as if they were glued to the ground.

'Our little deception has paid you well enough.'

'True, but it's a different matter my just being the physical body for your brains when we've only been doing business deals. Now you want something more. Something I don't understand.' O'Hara was scared.

The figure stepped closer.

'Vengeance. That's the word, Jason. Vengeance. I have spent half your lifetime reaching this moment. Why? Vengeance, Jason. You can never imagine the extent of Woodrow's poison and what it did to me. What it continues to do to me. I do not hide in this room because I like it. I remain here because this is the only place where my appearance cannot defile the eyes of the innocent. I will get my revenge. I have earned it. I shall not be denied its sweet nectar. You are my only chance of getting it, Jason.'

O'Hara felt the coldness of the creature before him chilling his bones as he tried to control his own terror. Yet for all his fears, O'Hara knew this once ordinary man who hid in the darkness of this room deserved the right to confront the obnoxious Jacob Woodrow.

'What should I do?'

'First you send Bates to Jacob Woodrow's home and invite the greedy swine here to receive his ten thousand dollars.' The figure moved to the chair hidden in the shadows and seated itself.

'And then?'

'Bring him here to my room and I shall do the rest, Jason.'

O'Hara nodded obediently. 'And what of Zococa?'

'We shall require our Mexican friend. He will make an ideal suspect for the sheriff to arrest when Jacob Woodrow's body is found, Jason.' The voice remained constant as it spoke. There was no hint of any emotion in its tone.

Jason O'Hara sighed heavily as he turned towards the slim shaft of light which indicated the doorway.

'I shall do everything exactly as you have instructed.'

'You are a good boy, Jason,' the voice said softly.

O'Hara nodded.

Conchita had seen the silent Tahoka many times over the years during which he had been Zococa's constant companion, but she had never seen him like this. Since returning alone to the cantina, he had brooded over the now cold bowl of chilli. Whatever were the thoughts or fears racing through his brain, Tahoka was cursed to keep to himself. Without anyone capable of understanding his talking hands, as Zococa could, the mute Apache was condemned to his own silent world.

Conchita had never felt totally at ease with the tall Apache until this warm evening. When he had walked in to be faced by the sheriff, she could feel the fear in his huge hand as she tried to lead him away from the probing questions. Although his face never seemed to change expression, she knew the big man had emotions lurking just below the surface.

'The horses are saddled and waiting out back, Tahoka,' she informed the quiet giant.

Tahoka's dark eyes turned towards the ravishing young woman as if he were vainly trying to communicate with her. His frustration caused him to shake his head.

'You are troubled, Tahoka?' The Apache nodded his head up and down slowly.

'You seem concerned that Zococa has not yet appeared within our humble cantina.' Conchita suddenly noticed that Tahoka was looking straight at her. The more intently she reciprocated the searching stare, the more she became aware of a peculiar tenderness in his tortured eyes.

'Go to Zococa,' Conchita urged.

Tahoka rose to his feet and hesitated for a moment as he looked down into the gorgeous face. He touched her long black hair before striding off through the cooking area of the cantina and out into the yard.

As his massive frame left the building, Conchita stood and looked at her mother, who had been watching them. The young woman walked silently to the side of Mamá Gomez with a curious look upon her face.

'A long time ago the smiling Zococa rescued that big Apache, my daughter,' the older woman said quietly as if not wishing her words to be overheard.

'This I know, *Mamá*,' Conchita said, resting her fingers upon her mother's shoulders as she watched the woman's hands skilfully working above a hotplate.

'Tahoka had his tongue ripped from his mouth by whoever it was who had staked him over an ant hill,' Mamá Gomez continued.

'This I also know, my mother.' Conchita sighed sorrowfully as she watched her mother shaping dough in her strong hands.

Mamá Gomez touched her daughter's chin with her floured hand and looked hard into the lovely face. There was an intensity in the older woman's expression which was seldom seen by anyone.

'They did other things to poor Tahoka, my daughter. Very bad things. It is said he is not a real man any more.'

Conchita could see the tears in her mother's eyes as she paused to look away. Only then did she realize what her mother meant and understood why the mute Indian was different from other men. For the first time in her short life Conchita felt sympathy for a gentle soul who could never be as other men.

As she rushed to the rear doorway of the cantina she heard the horses galloping off into the darkness. Leaning against the cool wall, Conchita wondered what she could have said or done if the tall warrior had not already departed. Then it dawned on her, there was nothing anyone could say or do.

FIFTEEN

Frank Wilson had wearily circled the large house three times without finding any way to penetrate its defences. It had been many years since he was last inside Jacob Woodrow's property but he still remembered the layout of the huge interior and knew exactly how to reach the bedroom of his sweetheart Beth. Yet for him to achieve that goal, he had to get inside.

The house now resembled a fortress, unlike the last time he had been here to visit. The rancher could not understand why things had altered so drastically. Yet none of this was anything to do with him. This was something which had grown like a canker in the mind of Woodrow.

Frank Wilson came slowly around the corner of the huge building and stood frustrated beneath his sweetheart's bedroom window again.

Looking up at the closed window and the light which shone out from it, Wilson felt helpless. The light danced over the leaves of

136

the outstretched tree-branches as if mocking him for his lack of imagination.

There was no way for someone of Wilson's build to scale the wall up to the high window. If ever a man deserved to be able to fly, it was him. He had tried every one of the ground-floor windows but they were all locked tight. He suspected they had been nailed by Jacob Woodrow. The rear door had been bolted as well as locked as if Woodrow suspected somebody might try to gain entrance one dark night, a night such as this.

There seemed nothing Wilson could do except watch the taunting light which filtered out above his head, attracting moths and other winged creatures to its illumination. Clenching his fists, Wilson walked silently through the garden towards the trunk of the great tree and tried to gain a fleeting glimpse of the woman he had loved since the moment they had first met as children.

Zococa could have reached the window, Wilson surmised. Men like him seemed to be able to do anything they wished, unlike muscle-bound ranchers.

Then to his left Frank Wilson heard the noise of someone at the tall chained gates.

Ducking down, he crawled through the untended overgrown grass until he had a perfect view not only of the gate but of the solid door of the house.

Bates was pulling at a bell-cord hanging at the side of the gates, which in turn was connected directly to the house. Each time the butler tugged on the cord, the faint sound of a bell echoed from inside the house. Wilson knelt in the long grass as he heard the bolts on the door being released and watched the figure he recognized stepping out, carrying a long-barrelled pistol in his right hand. Jacob Woodrow had changed considerably since the young man had last set eyes upon him. He had always been a self-centred individual but now he just appeared to be frightened. As Woodrow walked down to the gates his head continually jerked back and forth as if he feared every dark shadow that fell across his property.

Wilson crawled closer to the house as he watched Woodrow nearing the gates where the thin figure of Bates waited like a starched statue. As Jacob Woodrow arrived at the chains, the young man raised himself up and ran silently into the open doorway. Sweat ran down the face of the rancher as he pressed his back against the wall, just inside the door frame. His heart was beating at twice its normal rate as he tried to control his shaking body.

He was inside, Wilson thought, as a sudden wave of relief washed over him.

Should he lock and bolt the door to keep Jacob Woodrow out?

That would be no good. That would just trap him inside in the same way as Beth was trapped.

A hundred thoughts raced through his mind as he finally managed to gain the courage to peek carefully out at the gates and the two talking figures.

Neither man had spotted him entering this place. They had been too wrapped up in their own missions. Too busy eyeballing one another to notice him.

Wilson exhaled as he looked around the interior of the hall trying to get his bearings. It was as dark inside this place as it was out in the garden, he thought. Perhaps even darker. Yet nothing had changed since the last time he had set foot in here. Taking a deep breath, he ran towards the staircase and made his way up it two steps at a time. As he reached the wide landing he heard the door closing downstairs and he stopped moving. Glancing around, Wilson saw the small recess which he remembered from his childhood days; days when he played hide and seek in this huge house with Beth. Silently, the rancher made his way into the cramped space of the alcove as he heard the solid footsteps of Jacob Woodrow ascending the stairs behind him.

As he stood in the narrow space, Wilson prayed that the man carrying the long-barrelled pistol would not turn his head to the left. It was dark but perhaps not dark enough.

Zococa had lain motionless for nearly thirty minutes upon the polished wood-block floor of the huge dining-room within the heart of Jason O'Hara's home. Feeling as if his head had been in an argument with a grape-press, the bandit opened his eyes and stared blankly across the room. Everything seemed as if it were tilted sideways to his eyes, which slowly began to focus through the pain which throbbed like an Indian drum in his skull.

Gradually Zococa began to become aware of where he was and what had happened to him as he lay looking at the drying blood next to his face. His instincts told him to remain frozen as he tried desperately to fathom his situation more clearly. He had heard men talking somewhere away in the distance, heard voices which were cold and calculating.

Zococa blinked and began to focus on the objects in his line of sight. The legs of the long table stretched off into the distance directly before him. He soon gathered that he was lying in the middle of the dining-room and that he was not alone. Footsteps passed by him as if he were not there. Then he saw the shining black footwear of Bates pass before him and pause.

The bandit closed his eyes in case the butler might look down at the victim he had so easily clubbed. Then Zococa heard a heavier man entering the room, who stopped above his head.

'Well?' O'Hara's voice beckoned.

'It was so easy, sir. Woodrow took the bait exactly as you said he would.' Bates laughed.

Zococa felt the floor vibrate as the two men walked past him to the long table. He could hear drinks being poured and consumed.

'When will he be here?' O'Hara asked.

'Very soon, I imagine. He rushed back

into his house to get a coat.' Bates chuckled as he spoke.

'Excellent. Now go and wake the driver and prepare the large carriage.' The voice of the younger man seemed, to the ears of the prone Zococa, to move around the room.

'The carriage? I do not understand, sir,' Bates said honestly as he followed the bigger man.

'Tonight we will leave this place for ever,' O'Hara informed him.

'With our guest?' Bates glanced nervously in the direction of the large drapes which hid the secret room.

'Yes, Bates.'

'What of Zococa?' The butler waved a hand at the figure of the bandit still lying on the floor.

'We shall leave him here with the body of Jacob Woodrow.' Jason O'Hara repeated the words which had been branded into his mind.

'To take the blame?' Bates licked his thin lips.

'Exactly.'

Zococa listened to the two men laughing as they walked in different directions out of the room. Then he opened his eyes again. Blinking hard, Zococa forced himself up off the floor and onto his knees. The drums within his head grew louder as he held onto the back of a hard chair to steady himself. There was no time to waste, this he knew. With every ounce of his strength Zococa managed to claw himself up onto his feet. Once upright he stood, trying to stop the room from spinning before his eyes as he listened for any sign of either man returning.

It took two attempts before he managed to get his feet to obey his commands and walk to the long table. Resting both his hands upon the shining surface he stared at his reflection in the gleaming wood. It did not look the way Zococa normally looked, he noted. He looked like a man who has had his brains knocked loose inside his head. Then he remembered, that was what had actually happened.

Staring around he saw his silver-plated pistol lying on top of a napkin next to the tray of uneaten food. He picked it up and quickly checked that it was still loaded before cocking its hammer and gripping it in readiness.

Staggering to the door which led out into the garden, Zococa was even more confused than ever. Whatever was going on had taken a new twist. Jacob Woodrow was going to be executed, according to what he had over-heard. The great Zococa was meant to be blamed for the killing.

As he walked out into the blackness, Zococa could see the light coming from the stables where the opulent coach was being readied by Bates and the driver.

Zococa tried to retrace his steps back to the street along the side of the house. No light ever reached this place even during the day. Here no gardener's shears had pruned away at the dense bushes. Zococa pushed out blindly with his hands as he staggered towards the faint street lights.

With every step Zococa took, he felt his physical strength returning, but the noise inside his skull grew even louder and more painful.

As he stumbled down the long pathway and out onto the boardwalk, Zococa felt a hand upon his shoulder. Looking weakly around, he sighed in relief as he focused on the familiar features.

It was Tahoka.

'You do not know how glad I am to see you, my little elephant,' the bandit said, falling into his partner's arms.

SIXTEEN

After taking his third sip at the canteen, Zococa looked at the face of the Indian who was cradling him in his strong arms beside their two resting mounts. The bandit had never been in a situation like this before and certainly never had his skull creased by a gun barrel. It was a learning experience for the usually brash Zococa but one he was determined not to squander.

'Is my brain still inside my head, little one?' the bandit asked as he poured water over his black hair.

Tahoka inspected the back of Zococa's head and grunted before helping his partner to his feet. The Indian removed the sombrero carefully from Zococa's back and hung it from the saddle horn of the pinto stallion.

'I think we should ride to the rancho of Frank Wilson, *amigo*,' the Mexican said as he carefully gathered up his reins from the ground.

Tahoka waved his hands frantically, urging

his injured friend to forget about these people. The large silent man knew this was no place for someone of Zococa's carefree attitude. This was far more serious and deadly. His fingers spoke of the dangers this place held for them and how they ought to ride back over the border to safety. The bandit smiled at his friend, the way he always smiled when he was about to take the most perilous route.

Stepping into his stirrup, Zococa pulled himself up into the high saddle and rubbed the water from his face.

'You are probably right, my little rhinoceros. But we cannot just ride away. Think of our reputation. Think of all the little children who would not understand their heroes running across the border.' Zococa was desperately trying to convince himself as well as Tahoka that staying and probably ending up in a fight was a good idea.

Tahoka threw himself up onto his flame-faced black mount and shook his head in frustration. Yet as he looked at his injured but still smiling friend, he knew it was pointless resisting.

'I must warn *Señor* Wilson about what I have learned, Tahoka.'

The two riders spurred their horses and began riding down the almost deserted street. A swirling mist seemed to float a few inches off the ground, chilling the night air. They had ridden only about two hundred yards away from the O'Hara property, and were heading towards the outskirts of Rio Concho when Zococa noticed a solitary figure marching in the opposite direction along the dimly illuminated boardwalk. Unknown to either rider, they had just passed the notorious Jacob Woodrow.

Continuing into the darkness Zococa and his partner rode on until they passed by the distinctive gates of the Woodrow property. The gates had been left wide open by Jacob Woodrow in his haste to collect the $10,000 Jason O'Hara had agreed to pay him.

Pulling hard on his reins, Zococa turned his pinto around within the eddying shadows as his trusty partner slowed his horse to a halt beside him. For a moment the Apache brave looked around, trying to work out what had caught Zococa's keen eye.

Leaning across to the black gelding, Zococa tapped his friend's arm and pointed at the gates which had been left unchained and open by Jacob Woodrow in his hurry to get to the money he so desperately craved. Sitting astride his stallion, who was chomping at his bit, the bandit began to look about the dark street until he saw something which surprised him.

The huge plough-horse that Zococa knew belonged to the rancher Frank Wilson was standing a few dozen yards away, where it had wandered after being abandoned earlier. If the horse was here, it seemed a good bet Wilson was also somewhere close.

'This is very interesting, little one.' Zococa smiled as he rode across to the grazing animal.

Tahoka steered his mount after the bandit, curiously wondering what his partner meant.

'Do you not see, Tahoka? Our *amigo* must have ridden to town after we left him.' Zococa turned his pinto and rode slowly up to the open gates before dismounting. He tied his reins to the iron rods of the gate and rested a hand upon it, staring at the house bathed in darkness.

The Apache slid from his horse and tied his own reins to the tall iron gates as he watched his friend peering up at the Woodrow house.

'I know it sounds strange, but I think

148

Frank Wilson might have become brave like myself and gone into this place,' Zococa said as he watched the hands of the Apache replying.

Zococa shook his head.

'I am going in. Is the great Tahoka bold enough to follow?'

Tahoka did not require his friend to repeat himself and walked beside the bandit up the long winding pathway towards the front of the house. As they reached the door, it unexpectedly flew open, causing both men to draw their weapons.

The small figure of Beth Woodrow dashed out into the arms of Zococa. Her shocked expression soon vanished as she recognized the smiling face looking down at her.

'Why do you throw yourself into the arms of Zococa, my lovely little lady?'

'Zococa!' she exclaimed.

'What frightens you so, beautiful one?' Zococa asked as he holstered his pistol.

Her eyes flashed across to the tall Apache before returning to the face of the man who somehow filled her with an inner confidence, an emotion which Beth Woodrow had begun to think had been crushed from her once strong soul.

'It's Frank, Zococa. He's dying.'

Zococa held her shoulders as he stared deeply into her tear-filled eyes.

'Take us to our young *amigo*, Beth,' Zococa said.

The beautiful young girl led the pair inside the dark house and across the hallway to the foot of the wide staircase. Zococa struck a match, placed it to a candle and stared down at the injured body of Frank Wilson.

'Tahoka. See if you can help our friend,' Zococa uttered as he tried to shield the young woman from casting her eyes down onto her lover.

Tahoka knelt down quickly and began checking the unconscious rancher carefully. The large Apache warrior had learned many things from his tribe's medicine-man during his youth. Zococa knew if Wilson could be saved, Tahoka was the man to save him.

'Is he dead?' Beth sobbed as she hovered behind the bandit's back, trying to see what the large Apache was doing.

'How did this happen, lovely woman?' Zococa asked.

'My father unlocked the bedroom door to tell me he was going to see Jason O'Hara to be paid for selling me to him as a wife,' Beth's words poured out. 'The light from my room revealed Frank hiding in a corner of the landing. Frank tried to talk to my father but all my father wanted was to fight. Frank seemed unwilling to raise his fists in anger and took a terrible beating. Somehow Frank stumbled and fell down the stairs. My father rushed out to get his money.'

Zococa shook his head as he comforted the young woman.

Tahoka looked up into his partner's face. His expression gave nothing away. His hands spoke quickly and the Mexican nodded.

'My little Tahoka can help your sweetheart but it would be wise if you got a doctor to come and tend to his injuries,' Zococa told the shaking Beth.

Beth gulped and held the bandit's hands as she stared up into his handsome face.

'The nearest doctor is half-way across town, Zococa.'

'Take Tahoka's horse. His is most gentle and very swift.' The smiling bandit held her chin up with his fingers.

'But what are you going to do, Zococa?' she asked.

'I have to go to *Señor* O'Hara's house because I think your father is going to be killed.' His face suddenly went serious as he led her to the doorway. 'Do you wish for me to try and save the life of your father, Beth? I do not think he is a very nice man by what I have heard, but it is up to you.'

'But he is my father,' she said regretfully.

Zococa led her down the path to the waiting horses and helped her onto the black gelding before mounting his own pinto.

'Ride like the wind, little lady,' Zococa urged her as he spurred his own mount and thundered off into the distance.

SEVENTEEN

The face of Jason O'Hara drained of all colour as he strode into the large dining-room and realized Zococa was no longer lying on the floor. For a moment he just gazed around as if he might see the bandit if he tried hard enough. Cautiously stepping forward, O'Hara looked at the dried blood at his feet. A cold shiver overwhelmed him as he noticed the silver-plated pistol no longer rested upon the long dining-table.

As Bates walked into the room from the darkness of the garden, he saw the shocked expression carved into his master's face.

'Zococa's gone,' O'Hara announced, pointing at the wood-block floor. 'Did you see him out there?'

'I saw no sign of him as I came from the stables, sir.' The butler rushed across to his master, who seemed frozen to the spot, and stared blankly down at the red stain.

Jason O'Hara shook his head as terror surged through his veins and he began to realize how dangerous it was to lose track of an injured bandit like Zococa. An outlaw with his head split open.

'How the hell could he have even woken up after you parted his hair with that Colt?' O'Hara snarled angrily at his bewildered butler.

'I did hit him very hard. He must have the hardest head in Mexico.' Bates looked stiffly at the bloodstain which bore testament to the severity of his actions.

'We've got to find him fast,' O'Hara said, glancing at the wall-clock hanging above an array of candles. 'Woodrow will be here at any moment. We cannot risk that damn Mexican warning Woodrow before...'

'What I cannot understand, sir, is why you did not allow me to kill Jacob Woodrow when he was last here,' Bates said as he watched his pale-faced employer. 'It would have saved us so much trouble.'

'You forget, it is neither you nor I who wishes to kill Jacob Woodrow. It is him.' O'Hara pointed at the long drape which concealed the hidden door.

'But he could have done it yesterday when the greedy swine showed up,' Bates protested.

'You forget Woodrow showed up un-expectedly, Bates,' O'Hara said anxiously.

'Right now our main problem is Zococa. Our friend will see to Woodrow.'

Bates understood. He had been with O'Hara a long time but not as long as he had been with the man who hid himself from prying eyes and never allowed anyone to see his ever disintegrating features.

'Zococa might still be somewhere within the house, sir,' Bates said as he pulled the blood-stained pistol from his shoulder holster beneath his coat.

O'Hara moved closer to the manservant.

'If he's in here, find him, Bates. Find him quickly and kill him.'

'If he's in here, I'll find him, sir.' The butler began to smile. It was not a pretty sight and thankfully quite a rare occurrence.

Bates raised the cocked weapon until its cold steel rested against his cheek and made his way into the depths of the huge house. There were no shadows capable of frightening this man. He had lived too long with the knowledge hidden behind the secret door to be afraid of anything. If the bandit was within its confines, Bates would locate and execute him.

Jacob Woodrow had walked up the long dark pathway cautiously. He had been tricked many times by many people in his life and was not going to allow it to happen again. Pausing before the front door he pulled his Smith & Wesson Schofield .45 from the holster over his hip and checked it. It was a weapon that had served him well for more than a decade and he knew why it was reputedly Jesse James's first choice. Sliding the single-action revolver back into its well-oiled holster Jacob Woodrow reached down into his deep frock-coat pocket and found the small two-shot Remington .41 nestling in the silk fabric.

As he raised his fist and began knocking at the solid door he recalled how many card games had been won thanks to the small pistol. He had probably killed more men with the tiny gun than he had with the larger .45.

As the large door slowly opened, the eyes of Bates locked into those of Woodrow. Neither man cared for the sight of the other and it showed.

'My master is expecting you, Mr Woodrow,' the butler said quietly as he ushered the visitor into the house.

'Good. Very good.' Woodrow laughed as he pushed past the smaller man. 'Just take me to the money.'

Following the obnoxious figure of Jacob Woodrow into the glowing heart of the house, Bates narrowed his eyes and felt the gun beneath his left armpit. With every step he wished it was he who would be allowed to exterminate this human vermin. With every beat of his heart, he yearned to blast a hole in the back of the arrogant skull.

Bates cleared his throat loudly enough to make the strutting Woodrow turn round and stare at him.

'What?' Woodrow shouted.

The manservant walked towards the hanging drapes and pulled them away from the wall, revealing the secret door. For a moment the eyes of the older man wrinkled up in confusion as he looked at the door.

'What's this?' Woodrow asked the impassive butler.

Bates turned the handle and pushed the door inwards. He forced a smile.

'My master is waiting with your money inside, sir.'

'I don't get it.' Woodrow felt uneasy as he looked at the door.

'You do not seem the sort of man who fears anything, Mr Woodrow.' Bates waved a hand at the open door. 'I'm not afraid of anything,' Jacob Woodrow snapped as he stepped towards the butler and the drapes.

'My master is within waiting with the money, sir. This is a secret room where he keeps all his cash and important papers.' Bates waited as Woodrow glared at him before stepping into the darkness. Faced with a blackness he had not expected, Woodrow turned on his heels only to see and hear the door slamming behind him.

The sound of its key being turned in the lock sent shock waves of panic racing through his body. Jacob Woodrow grabbed at the door-handle and rattled it frantically as his eyes tried vainly to penetrate the darkness.

'At long last, Jacob.' The haunting voice seemed to float over the terrified figure of Woodrow like a liquid poison. As he turned and looked into the nothingness that faced him, Woodrow remembered where he had heard the voice before. Suddenly, he felt horror overwhelming him.

EIGHTEEN

Zococa stood in the stirrups of the thundering stallion as he closed in on the house of Jason O'Hara. The sight of the solitary figure holding the scatter-gun across his broad chest, blocking his way, stunned the bandit. Reining in, Zococa hauled the huge horse to a standstill within inches of the unblinking sheriff.

Controlling the rearing animal beneath him, Zococa faced the lawman with a sense of bewilderment.

'Hold up, Zococa,' Bob Barker said down the length of the shotgun.

Zococa looked down at the man who wore a star.

'I am in a hurry, Sheriff.'

Barker waved his gun confidently.

'Dismount or I'll kill you where you sit, boy.'

Zococa quickly got off his horse and moved towards the solid sheriff who was keeping his weapon trained upon the elusive bandit. Looking across at the house of Jason

O'Hara, Zococa began to wonder how long Beth Woodrow's evil father had left to live if he could not intervene.

'I must go, *señor*. It is a matter of life and death.'

Barker shook his head as he stared hard into the face of the man he had chased so unsuccessfully for so many years. It was dark and hard to see anything clearly but the sheriff knew this just had to be the man he had hunted for so long.

'You are Zococa. I know you are.'

'My name is Luis Santiago Rodrigo Vallencio, *amigo*.' Zococa smiled as he walked within a few feet of Barker. 'I think you have made the mistake.'

Barker shook his head. 'Take the gun out of your holster with two fingers, boy.'

Zococa felt helpless as he stared down the long barrel of the scatter-gun. Reluctantly the still-smiling bandit held onto his gun-grip and began pulling it from his holster when the sound of another gun firing made both men spin around in the direction of the large house.

Sheriff Barker gasped in disbelief as the sound of yet another shot echoed into the night air. As Bob Barker looked back to Zococa, his mouth fell open.

The bandit had gone.

The house was quiet again as Zococa entered quickly, holding his trusty silver-plated pistol firmly in his favoured left hand. He ran in through the open front doorway and knelt down as he tried to work out where the occupants were. There was no sign of anyone for a few heartbeats, then he saw the two figures beyond the narrow passageway in the large dining-room. A room where he had left a pint of his blood earlier.

Zococa rose, gritted his teeth and moved forward quickly and silently until he was standing just inside the brightly illuminated room. The two men did not notice him at first as he leaned against the wooden framework watching them.

'Zococa!' exclaimed Jason O'Hara, pointing feverishly over the head of Bates, who was seated.

Both men seemed totally shocked by the sight of the man they had tried so desperately to find only a few minutes earlier.

O'Hara rushed across the room towards a tall cabinet and frantically tried to open its massive doors. Zococa aimed and fired his pistol quickly, sending a thousand splinters showering over the startled man.

'Do not try and find yourself a gun, *señor*. This would be most unwise, I think,' Zococa said calmly as he pulled his gun-hammer back once more.

It was Bates who drew his weapon from under his arm and fired accurately at the smiling bandit. The bullet hit Zococa squarely in his chest, sending him falling backwards.

'You got him,' Jason O'Hara cried in relief as he dragged the doors of the cabinet open and pulled out a loaded Winchester rifle.

Bates began to take aim again at the stricken bandit when the taller man moved next to him cocking the carbine.

'I want to finish him, Bates,' O'Hara said, eagerly raising the heavy weapon to his shoulder.

'Be my guest, sir.' Bates sighed.

Zococa rolled over onto his elbow and blasted a fast shot off at the looming figure of O'Hara. The tall man staggered into the butler and fell onto his knees before realizing his life had ceased. The blood began to stream from the middle of his white shirt as he fell across the feet of the shocked butler.

Bates cocked his pistol and stared into the

cloud of gunsmoke which marred his view of the bandit. Then his attention was drawn to the figure beyond Zococa rushing towards the dining-room. All he could see for sure was the lamplight catching the sheriff's star as he continued coming at him. Firing quickly at the lawman, Bates ran over to the cover of the large padded couch before squeezing his trigger once more.

Barker rolled over the top of Zococa and slid under the long dining-table before letting rip with both barrels of his scatter-gun. The impact of the lead shot tore the seat to ribbons, sending horse-hair padding flying out in all directions. Bates rose to his feet and aimed straight at the lawman as he expelled his spent shotgun shells.

The snarling butler felt the thudding blow hitting him in his side before he heard the sound of the silver-plated gun being fired. It was like being kicked by a horse. Bates was thrown crashing into the solid wall behind him by its sheer force. His gun hit the floor and fired a wayward bullet off into the wood flooring. Bates neither saw nor heard that final shot. He was dead before his body reached the ground.

Bob Barker slid two shotgun shells into his rifle and snapped it shut before slowly getting up from beneath the cover of the table. He stepped over O'Hara's body before satisfying himself Bates was no longer in the land of the living. The room was filled with choking gunsmoke and couch-stuffing, which hung in the air. Walking across towards the bandit, he began to wonder what on earth was taking place.

'You saved my life, Zococa,' Barker drawled as he looked down at the bandit with the smouldering bullet hole in his jacket, directly level with his heart.

'It was an accident, *amigo*.' Zococa smiled as he allowed the sheriff's free hand to pull him off the floor.

Barker stared at the hole in Zococa's jacket.

'How come you ain't dead, boy?'

Zococa reached into his jacket and pulled out his silver cigar-case. The bullet was flattened into its centre.

'I think it is lucky for me that I stole this case, *señor*.'

Before the sheriff could speak again, a haunting scream came from behind both men. Barker pushed past the bandit and glanced around before noticing the hem of the heavy drape.

'You see what I see, Zococa?'

The bandit rubbed his bruised chest and tilted his head.

'I see the bottom of a door, *amigo*.'

'That's what I see, boy.' Barker grabbed the drape and tore it away from the wall. Several years of dust fell over the two men as they looked at the door.

'I think the scream came from within there, Sheriff,' Zococa said as he watched the lawman nervously turning the key before gripping the handle.

'Cover me?' Barker asked as he raised the scatter-gun barrel up in the air.

Zococa smiled broadly and nodded.

'It would be an honour, Sheriff.'

Taking a deep breath, Barker twisted the handle and entered the dark room. Lowering the rifle to waist height, the sheriff stood trying to see inside. Then he noticed the body of Jacob Woodrow lying on the floor a few feet away from the tip of his square-toed boots.

Zococa stepped in beside the motionless sheriff and squinted at the shimmering figure trying to hide in the corner of the room. The bandit immediately knew the figure was not hiding from them but from the lamplight which stretched across the dust-covered floor.

'*Amigo*?' Zococa said to the figure who huddled in the darkest part of the room.

'Is it a man, Zococa?' Bob Barker asked as he knelt down beside the body of Jacob Woodrow.

'I'm a man. Or at least I once was,' a voice replied from beneath its heavy robes.

Zococa looked at the sheriff who seemed puzzled by the body on the floor.

'What's wrong, my friend?'

'This is Jacob Woodrow. He'd dead OK but there ain't a mark on the critter.' Barker rose back to his full height and rubbed his whiskered chin.

The bandit stepped over the corpse and looked at its face. It was wide-eyed and open-mouthed. Zococa had never seen such an expression on anyone living or dead.

'How did you kill him, *señor*?' Zococa stepped closer to the shape in the corner.

'I did not lay a hand upon him,' the voice replied. 'He did however shoot me.'

Zococa looked at the sheriff and then back at the figure who seemed so desperate to conceal his appearance from them. His fingers pointed down at the blood which led to the strange figure opposite.

'You are wounded?' Barker asked loudly.

The figure managed to stand but kept

166

close to the wall.

'Woodrow's done for me, men. But not before I saw him die the way I had planned.'

'But he's not marked,' the sheriff said.

'You could say he died of fright. I scared him to death.' The voice seemed to be getting weaker with every word which came from beneath the loose shapeless shroud.

'Should we get you a doctor, *señor*?' Zococa asked.

'No. I must die. I had become as bad as Jacob Woodrow over the years as I tried to seek revenge for what he did to me.'

'What did he do to you, mister?' Bob Barker questioned.

The shape staggered along the wall before pausing.

'He made me a monster. It was long ago and we had been partners for a short while. The trouble was Woodrow had a way of using partners up in quick fashion. I bore the consequences and he disappeared with the profits. I had no idea of what he had done until I began to change from being a normal man and started to change into something not fit to be looked upon by innocent eyes.'

'What exactly did he do, man?'

The figure slid down to the floor.

'It does not matter. Let us just say he sowed the seeds of my demise long ago. So long ago he forgot all about me and what he had done to me. Just as he blocked all his evil deeds out of his mind. The slaves he used and killed. The wife he killed to get her family fortune. Woodrow had a way of destroying everything just to keep himself rich. He always managed to forgive himself though. He was good at forgiving himself until tonight.'

Zococa holstered his gun.

'Was it you who wanted me to kill Frank Wilson?'

'Yes. I had this crazed idea that if you killed Wilson we could easily make the sheriff here believe you had also killed Jacob Woodrow. But I was wrong. I had succumbed to the pain of my affliction.' The voice grew even weaker.

'How did you kill Woodrow, mister?' Barker wondered aloud.

'I allowed him to strike a match and let him see my face.'

Zococa shook his head sadly.

'What is your name, *amigo*?'

'My name? Monsters have no name, Zococa. But once I was called Jason O'Hara.'

168

Barker and the bandit glanced at one another.

'The man out there was merely an actor I hired long ago when I first started to become too hideous to walk the streets. I required someone who could execute my business dealings for me without scaring the pants off folks.' The voice now was a mere whisper.

Zococa stepped closer to the figure upon the floor.

'What can I do for you, *señor*?'

'You wish to help me, Zococa? In God's name why?' The voice broke.

'I think you have rid the world of a very bad man,' Zococa responded. 'For this alone, I think we owe you something.'

'I would ask you to light an oil lamp and place it next to me and then leave this house,' the voice gasped painfully.

Zococa turned and looked at the sheriff. Barker nodded and walked out of the room only to return carrying a glass globe-lamp which he handed to the bandit.

Zococa placed it on the floor and removed the glass globe before striking a match and touching the moist wick.

'Now leave,' the voice ordered.

As Barker and Zococa closed the front

door of the large house and walked down to the silent street they said nothing. Turning to face the house, they stood shoulder to shoulder as the flames began to lick the night sky.

Engulfed in a fiery inferno, its secrets were soon nothing more than smoke and ashes.

FINALE

Tahoka rode along the street just after the sun began to rise over the small sleeping town of Rio Concho. The house was now only rubble and smouldering ashes where once two very different men calling themselves Jason O'Hara had lived. It seemed to the watching men that the flames had purified countless evils. As the proud Apache reined his mount up beside the pinto stallion he could not quite believe the sight before him.

Zococa was standing next to the broad-shouldered Bob Barker watching the smoke rising into the cloudless morning sky.

'I see the dish-washer has arrived, Zococa,' the sheriff noted.

'Is our friend Frank Wilson OK, little rhinoceros?' Zococa smiled at his partner.

Tahoka nodded.

'Remember, Sheriff. There is oil on the land of Frank Wilson and he does not know how rich this can make him,' Zococa said to the lawman as he ran a hand down the nose of his horse.

'I'll make sure he finds out,' Barker said as he watched the Mexican stepping into his stirrup and mounting his powerful stallion.

'Please make sure he marries the lovely Beth too,' Zococa grinned as he placed his sombrero onto his still sore head and gathered up his reins.

'You still didn't say why you shot that butler when he was going to kill me, Zococa.' Barker rubbed his neck as he looked up at the grinning bandit.

'I did not like the man, *señor*. He broke my head and tried to kill me.' Zococa laughed as Tahoka drew his horse level with his pinto.

'Is that the real reason?' Bob Barker rested his knuckles on his hips and looked up at the strange pair of riders above him.

'Also, I thought it would be a crime to allow such a handsome man as yourself to be shot by a man who looked like a very sick racoon.' Zococa tapped his spurs into his horse began to allow his mount to walk down the street away from the man wearing the star.

'Hey, Zococa...' Barker called out.

'But, Sheriff. My name is Luis Santiago Rodrigo Vallencio, not Zococa. Is it not so, my little elephant?' Zococa winked.

Tahoka nodded as he drew his flame-faced gelding alongside his laughing partner. Both riders slapped their reins and began galloping down the long street heading south towards the nearby border. Looking up, Bob Barker caught sight of the figure of Donna Drumbar heading towards him faster than he had ever seen her move before.

He began smiling. *'Adios,* Zococa. Next time…'